I0658517

MOON CREEK PUBLISHING FIRST EDITION,
MARCH, 2014

ISBN: 978-0-9915925-0-0

Book Design by Del Boland
Cover Design by Del Boland

Printed in the United States of America
U.S. Copyright Registration Number
TXu 1-891-660

www.delboland.com
http://twitter.com/delboland
https://www.facebook.com/mooncreekpublishing

ACKNOWLEDGEMENTS: My thanks to the following for your inspiration:

To God, without whom, nothing is possible.

To my close family, especially Anne, Jacob, David, Betty, Bosky, and Dee. Anne, you're my light and my rock. Jacob, you're one of the great joys in my life. Dee, if I had the opportunity to pick a sister, I'd pick you.

Alice Weathers, Pat Wood, Jimmy Swearingen et. al., Gary Swearingen, Sharon Davis, Jimmy Ratliff, Jeannie Hogland, Pam Davis, Donnis Strickland, Pat Williams, Maderia Naten, Sheila Dismuke and the Bolands, I'm always proud we're part of the same family.

Bill Pursley the RFG. Don't know what I woulda done without you, brother. Oh, and Kathleen for keeping me alive during the lean years.

The Augusta gang, especially my good friend, Randy Roberts.

Marty Weathersby, Jim Elick, Dave Sewell, Nelson Miranda and Doug Stull, my bandmates in Blue Kudzu. What a crazy, fun enterprise! Miss ya'll.

Lans Rothfusz, Kathy Rothfusz, Gary Pederson, the Kahleys, the Summers, the Callisons and other members of

GraceFlock, I gained so much from our time together. Also, Pastor John Weber.

Pastor Gary Peterson and everyone at Word of Life, God bless you.

CRHP 28 and Chris McKenzie, Cornerstone Cafe (and Maureen who might have contributed at least one catch phrase), everyone at Good Shepherd, especially Pastors Gary Olson, Greg Wenhold, Glen Wagner, and PJ Malin.

Linda Yoakam, Don Heller, Linda Heller, Kathy Blackburn, Kathy Krivacek, the Plaskotas, Dave and Laura Schubert, Jeff Ruge, Thrivent Financial Cantera (esp. Zac Larson, Corey Schmidt), Steve Boisse, PACT, Inc., and We Grow Dreams.

The folks at Naperville Writer's Group for all the great commentary and snarky wisdom.

Kasie Marie Smith for realizing that Bill could not have a peanut allergy on page 46 and then order a peanut butter and jelly sandwich on page 165.

Best selling author, Cara Lockwood, for your editing expertise. Karen Lankisch and Glen Veed for the initial shove.

A special thanks to the angels in my life, Mom, Dad, Dr. Bompart, Aunt Irene, Aunt Leona, Aunt Ruby, Harold, Aunt Mattie Lee, Uncle Leonard, Forrest, Billy, Donna and Uncle Bubba.

Del Boland

HOMELAND INSECURITY

A novel by Del Boland

"Rightful liberty is unobstructed action according to our will within limits drawn around us by the equal rights of others."

Thomas Jefferson

Del Boland

BERNIE

Pick up uniform from laundry. Check. Flowers for mom's birthday. Check. Buy apples, kielbasa and cabbage. Check.

He clicked each completed item on his smart phone app, then wriggled the device into the front pocket of his jeans as he sat on an upside-down, five-gallon bucket, peering through an open window.

Retrieving a Granny Smith apple from his backpack, he wiped it on his shirt, admiring dense clusters of daffodils planted among patches of grass across the street at Brookhaven Park. Dappled light danced on the ground, projected through a canopy of shimmering new foliage from the surrounding trees.

Two chattering preschoolers hung from monkey bars at a playground. He smiled as the two black boys jumped down and ran toward him, stopping at the edge of the park, lingering on the opposite side of the road from the abandoned apartment building where he watched from the second floor.

Bernie bit into his apple, looking down as they searched the grass on both sides of the sidewalk, perhaps looking for treasure, each with their back turned to the other. Holding the apple between his teeth, Bernie lifted a golf-ball-sized piece of broken plaster from the floor, extended his left arm for balance and threw it across the narrow lane, hitting the larger boy between the shoulders, the white chunk of lime and sand breaking into pieces on the sidewalk.

"Sammy!!"

Sammy, oblivious to the charge, turned in time for his friend's shove, toppling both boys onto the grass, wrestling and shouting. The larger boy gained an advantage on top, pinning Sammy's arms, hitting him twice in the face with his fist. The smaller boy began to cry.

"Life ees not *fair* leetle boy. Get *used* to eet," Bernie muttered.

Bernie took another bite from the apple before tossing it through the window with a gloved hand, the core landing on the sidewalk fourteen feet below.

Next to Bernie, a fifteen-speed bicycle leaned against a graffiti covered wall along with his backpack from which he'd retrieved and unfolded the weapon in less than ten seconds. He could fold and store it in three seconds.

The Ruger Mini 14, chosen after months of research for its light weight and efficiency, rested on the window sill. Bernie lifted the butt end of the rifle, closed one eye and peered briefly through the scope at Sammy's tear streaked face — the boy now sitting in the grass.

Bernie pulled a small cloth from his pocket and wiped the lens on the scope —assessing. On the opposite corner, a black man had emerged from a narrow alley next to Papa Joe's Grocery, an old community store with boarded windows. Wearing faded jeans, T-shirt and a red, yellow and green tam, the man leaned his back against the brick wall and propped up a green sneakered foot.

It was the fourth time in ten months. Mapping his escape route, he'd ridden his bicycle to a van parked five or six blocks away, few noticing the casual way he rode away from each scene. By the time they'd muster the courage to go inside a vacant building, he was long gone through the back. Bernie had watched the evening news and read the papers on the days following. One of the shootings wasn't reported at all.

Bernie noted the time on his watch.

He nestled the butt of the rifle against his shoulder and pressed his cheek against the stock, aligning the crosshairs on his target. He began to squeeze. A truck rumbled in the distance along the main road dividing the apartment building from the grocery. He eased the pressure on the trigger, waiting for the truck to pass, then squeezed again —tighter, tighter, until the familiar, piercing *BOOM*! He ejected the brass casing on the floor where it would remain, the letters KKK engraved on the side.

The man slid down, his tam askew on his head, blood trailing down the wall. Someone yelled as Bernie calmly folded the gunstock and placed the rifle into the pack. He tossed it over one shoulder and jogged down the steps holding the bicycle on his other shoulder.

Out back, a homeless man staggered, looking down at an old, grass-covered brick walkway which connected the back door of the building to the alley, an unforeseen complication. Lowering the bike, Bernie slid his wraparound sunglasses over his eyes from their perch on top of his head, then strapped on his helmet, considering his options while watching the man through the door. He reached into the front pocket of his pants, feeling the handle of a folded razor, and then wheeled the bicycle across the rotted threshold.

"*Hey* man, gotta *dolla*?" The man's murky eyes followed Bernie's hand fishing a crinkled bill from his front pocket. A twenty. Bernie waved it low, then tossed it on the ground with his gloved hand.

"God bless you," the old man said, grabbing the money with dirty fingers.

Bernie walked with the bicycle to the alley, hopped on and leisurely pedaled away from the intersection.

LIB

"*Cheese*borger, *cheese*borger!" Tony shouted, placing his order at the counter.

Lib sat at a table, eyeing the lunch crowd of mostly local businessmen, waiting on Tony. He delivered his Diet Coke and chips to the table. No Pepsi. "Was that really necessary?" she asked.

"You've never seen the SNL skit?"

"Of course. Everybody in Chicago has."

They sat amid dozens of newspaper articles posted on the walls describing the adventures of founder Billy Sianis and his famous goat at the Billy Goat Tavern. They'd walked down the steps onto the dark sidewalk before stepping sixty years back in time, surrounded by checkered table tops and brightly colored '50s style chairs.

She read one of the articles, waiting as Tony trotted back for his double cheeseburger at the call of his name. He didn't ask if she wanted anything.

Returning, he plopped in his chair, a bite already removed from the sandwich en route.

"You believe the curse?" she asked.

"Sure, don't you?" he responded, one cheek bulging.

"I guess so, after so many years."

He sipped his pop and looked at her. "They shoulda let Sam's goat go to all the games. In fact, they shoulda given 'em both a box . . . paid for 'em to attend away games."

"Yeah, *right*! The Cubs *suck*, goat or *no* goat."

Tony's face, an unfortunate barometer of his moods, turned red — part of a familiar routine in which she'd remind him about the 2005 White Sox and he'd defend his Cubs. She didn't fit the White Sox stereotype — she just liked watching his face change colors.

Directing his gaze at the tanned space between her breasts, the color of his face returned to its natural ruddy state. "So, who drove in the winning run?"

She shifted in the red vinyl chair then leaned her face down into his line of sight, "Excuse me?"

"Who drove in the winning run for the Sox in 2005?" he repeated to her breasts as she sat back up.

Two seconds passed.

Five.

He grinned and looked up at her face. She showed no expression.

"Geoff Blum," she said quietly.

Her lips parted, revealing the smile she used to disarm her opponents. He laughed. "Luck," he said under his breath.

Lib watched Tony chomp his way through the cheeseburger with mechanized efficiency, devouring and flushing burger mash into his body with intermittent slurps of pop.

"I don't know how you eat this stuff every day," she said.

He swept his arm in an arc like Vanna White demonstrating a holiday package on Wheel of Fortune. "You kidding? This is one of the best restaurants in Chicago."

She sighed. "You should try Alinea."

Tony scooped a gob of ketchup into his mouth with a

cluster of crinkle cut fries. "I've heard about that place," he mumbled. "They serve tiny spoons of chemicals for a half K."

Draining the last of his pop, Tony swept the end of his straw around the bottom of the cup, appearing unfazed by the slurping noise, drawing the attention of a man and woman seated at the next table.

Lib propped an elbow on her folded arm, pressing the edge of her flattened hand against one side of her face in mock embarrassment, rolling her eyes for added effect. "It's deconstructed," she said. "They received three stars from Michelin."

"What the hell does a *tire* company care about finger food? And, if they're so great, how come they don't get *five* stars?"

"Three stars is the highest rating you can get."

"Who ever heard of three stars as the highest rating? That's just *wrong*!"

Tony crammed the last of his fries into his mouth, rolling the wrappers into a ball on the table.

"Forget it," she said.

Tony stood and tossed the wadded paper in the garbage on the way to the door, Lib following close behind.

They exited the restaurant on Lower Wacker and climbed the stairs to Michigan Avenue, putting on shades and walking toward the Tribune building. Winter was officially over, but the wind felt cold on Lib's face in the shadow of the parking deck.

Entering the stairwell, they rushed past the urine smell, taking two stairs at a time to the second level, finding Tony's '69 Camaro. He didn't bother to open the door for her.

Inserting his key and turning, the engine echoed through the concrete structure, mixed with the sounds of other cars from the street below.

She glanced into the back seat at a collection of fast food bags as Tony maneuvered the car down to street level.

Though a little on the heavy side, Tony was actually a good-looking guy with blondish, wavy hair cut a little long for a man his age. He had a rugged appearance with perpetual stubble outlining what could be a very nice beard. His teeth were a little crooked in front, but overall, not bad at all.

The power of the old muscle car pressed her back against the seat as Tony pulled out of the parking deck through tight traffic onto State Street.

Lib cracked a window, diluting the concentration of mildew and other airborne pathogens — the result of rain that had leaked through several holes in the convertible top. Dangling shreds of canvas flapped in the sunlight as Tony passed a bus.

"I plan to refurb everything. New seats, new carpet, new top." She nodded at the oft repeated line.

He drove along LaSalle past Daley Center.

"You missed your turn."

"Let's stop by my place, I need a tie."

She surveyed his wrinkled, short sleeve button down and stained khakis. A tie would add little value.

Tony moved along with traffic, waving at some kids playing on the sidewalk in Wicker Park. "You know them?" she asked.

"Yeah." He drove several more blocks before turning into an alley, parking behind an old Cape Cod.

"I'll just sit in the car," she said.

"Suit yourself." He got out and pressed his six two frame through an opening in the fence.

She looked around then stepped out, turning sideways

through a rusty gate hanging by a single hinge before catching up to him near the top of the metal stairs. An old door with peeling white paint separated them from the finished attic space he called home.

Using separate keys to unlock two deadbolts, he opened the door and walked inside. She stepped into the efficiency apartment behind him, waiting for her eyes to adjust near the door.

He tossed clothes onto an unmade bed, gesturing for her to sit on a cluttered love seat nearby. She stood, refusing contact with anything in the stuffy room, assessing a collection of men's magazines tossed inside two stacked milk crates which served as a nightstand between the seat and the bed.

"You know, we've got an hour before the mayor's press meeting," he said, winking.

"Get your tie and let's go. My skin's starting to itch."

"Can't blame a guy for *tryin'*."

"You have some nerve."

She watched him fumble around in a drawer then noticed the pistol on top of an old dresser.

"Okay, Mr. *Gun* Control, what's with the revolver?"

He worked to untangle a nest of neck ties before retrieving an outdated dark maroon number with geometric designs. "Yeah, well . . . ," he said, " . . . you can't be too careful these days."

"So, it's okay for you to have a gun?"

"No. I mean . . . ,"

"No worries. I've got a Glock 9 mm," she announced, looking around at more peeled paint on the walls. "I bought it when the shootings started."

His tie draped around his neck, Tony lifted the nickel plated gun. "It's a Smith and Wesson .38 that belonged to my dad." He offered it to her. She waved him off.

"What did Joe hear about Mayor Epstein?" she asked. Tony worked on the tie, standing in front of a small mirror hung on the wall.

"Somehow, they captured some video," he said, threading the small end through a half Windsor knot, his chin up.

"Is this one of those stories that takes all our time and delivers nothing?"

"I don't think so. Epstein's planning a more aggressive response to the murders."

"He's already ordered police to stop and frisk," she added.

Tony knitted his eyebrows. "This is Chicago. He's the *mayor*. He does whatever he wants."

"The ACLU's all over him for profiling."

He tightened the knot and shrugged. "So?"

"What if *we* were the target? I think this's going a bit too far."

"I don't care *what* he does, as long as it restores order."

TOM AND GEORGE

"Hey Tom, check it out."

George posed beneath the Washington Street sign outside of Daley Plaza.

"Wait, let me get a picture," Tom said, struggling with ancient hands to control an electronic device.

An unusually tall, black woman sauntered past then stopped, studying Tom, her chin tucked back and large hands on her narrow hips. "*Hey* sugar britches, need some *help*?"

Tom stared at her pink sequined high heels, then followed her long legs in fishnet stockings up to her shiny pink shorts.

With a smirk, she extended one hand for the camera. "Go get in the picture wit your beau."

Tom handed the camera over, sidling next to George.

"*Work* it girls." She paused, peeking around the device. "C'mon, *smile*."

"We *are* smiling," George said, his thin lips pressed together in a straight line.

"Whatever. Say '*spank* me cowboy."

She snapped two shots then handed the phone back to Tom, coyly smiling at George. "Love the ensemble, sugar. Manly, yet delicate." He wore black riding boots over tan knee britches, a traditional colonial shirt with ruffled sleeves topped off with a blue Cubs hat.

"Yes, well, thank you," George said, managing a slight

upward curve on one side of his otherwise linear mouth.

Wearing a blue, green and orange Hawaiian shirt and black Bermuda shorts with his long white hair in a ponytail, Jefferson peeked over a pair of blue rectangular sunglasses slid down on his prominent nose as the woman sashayed across Daley Plaza, her matching pink handbag held head high.

"I think you could use a makeover, Georgie."

"What's a makeover?"

"You work with clothiers to find the right look. You need to catch up with the times, my dear sir."

George looked down at himself, thin lips pressed together. "What's wrong with the way I look?"

"That tall girl?"

"Yes."

"She was a *man*."

"*No*."

Tom nodded his head, still looking over his glasses.

"I saw her looking at your butt."

"*No*."

Tom nodded his head again.

"Things have changed," George said.

"You should run for president."

"I think we've had enough sightseeing for one day. It's time to get back to work."

"Still on the honesty kick, eh?" Tom said.

"We need to keep up with Michael. I don't want him to screw up."

George and his friend Tom vanished into the crowd.

TONY

"I want to begin by emphasizing the need for calm. We'll catch this guy."   Mayor Jay Epstein paused. "However, it's important to increase awareness, so we want to share what we know with the public."

He turned his head away from the microphones and coughed.

"Excuse me for one second."   Epstein stepped to one side of the podium and cleared his throat. He lifted a glass of water from the small table and drank half of it before resuming his position behind the usual array of microphones. The room was plain except for the Chicago city seal on the wall behind him and gray folding chairs arranged in front, occupied by a small gathering of reporters.

"Okay. Our profilers are working around the clock with possible witnesses. We're also going through surveillance footage in and around the areas where the shootings occurred."

The mayor turned his head and cleared his throat again.

"We believe we're looking for a man with dark hair and an accent," he rasped. "This person may exhibit any number of odd behaviors."

The mayor coughed and stopped to take another drink before continuing.

"The gun is a Ruger Mini 14 with a scope. The man may be riding a bicycle. We're urging everyone to report anything suspicious. The number is 877 357 2263." A moment of silence signaled his conclusion.

"Mr. Mayor. Tony Wochowski from the Tribune. Do you think this person is somehow linked to a terrorist organization?"

A few cameras flashed and clicked.

"Absolutely not. This is the act of a single individual with serious anger issues."

"Mayor Epstein. Lib Rand, also from the Tribune. With Chicago's new gun registration policy, is it possible we have this person on file?"

More cameras flashed.

"That's a good question, Lib. Unfortunately, I can only speculate that the person's not in our system, though our guys are cross checking every source at their disposal. I'm sure you're aware that I support a complete ban on firearms. I believe it's the only way to ensure protection."

Several hands jabbed in the air, the relative quietness of the room giving way to murmuring, a few calling the mayor's name, hoping to get their question in.

The mayor raised his voice slightly. "For the moment, our *job* . . . " The mayor looked at everyone gathered in the room. "No. Strike that. Our responsibility. Our responsi*bil*ity is to gather information from the public that'll help us catch this guy."

The mayor turned and walked through the door as several reporters called after him.

"Well, that was comforting," Lib said, gathering her iPad and purse from a chair.

Tony looked at her. "What did you expect?"

They walked away from the podium toward a double door at the back of the room, now open.

"The mayor's gotta send a message of calm resolve, but it had the opposite effect on me. I think things'll get a whole lot worse before they get better," she said.

"What does that mean?"

"We've disturbed a delicate balance between liberty and

tyranny."

Tony cut his eyes at her. "Your job is to report the news, not offer political views. Besides, if *you're* so smart, why don't *you* run for office?"

She smirked, revealing a dimple on one side of her face

"It's not about smart. I like the truth. I'd never survive."

"I agree with you on that point."

They filed out of the press room into the lobby of Daley Center, an uninspired rectangular building built in the '60s from rust covered Corten Steel.

Lib and Tony both checked their phones. Lib typed in a text.

"What's with the *guy*?" Tony asked. A man in a dark suit gazed boldly at them from across the open room.

"I don't know, maybe we should ask him." Lib walked toward the man who turned and stepped through double glass doors leading outside, disappearing on the busy sidewalk bordering Washington Street. "Probably just checking you out," Tony offered.

"Yeah, *right*."

She regularly drew the attention of men — usually the wrong kind, by his estimates.

Thinking of his mildly suggestive comment at the apartment, Tony gritted his teeth. Working together had certain advantages, but stepping over the line could create tension. He'd gotten to know her, maintaining a professional distance, fighting the urge to ask her out. She'd not said anything, so maybe she'd dismissed it.

She wasn't really his type anyway. She'd attended Harvard and spoke three languages. He'd worked his way through Columbia. She was a card totin' Libertarian. He was apolitical and apathetic. Like many Chicagoans, he'd resigned himself to accept the long-standing political machine.

Lib would never understand Chicago. Her father was a successful farmer and she was his only child — his pride and joy and the desire of every farm boy for miles around Lowell, Indiana, where she'd been Homecoming Queen and Valedictorian.

Tony recalled her long, beautiful legs that first day at the Trib and her wavy black hair pulled back neatly with a stylish hair clip, but it was her smile that rendered him incapable of forming a complete sentence when introduced. He'd stammered several inane comments — immediately trying to impress her. She'd just smiled and walked to the next row of cubicles with the editor.

Normally, the Ivy League guys got the beautiful interns. Yet, she was assigned to Tony, perhaps for protection. He was the tough guy. *They expected ME to protect HER?* he thought. *She didn't need protection. THEY needed protection.*

They walked outside into the sunlight. "I just can't help thinking that we're going in the wrong direction," she said.

"No, my car is this way."

"I'm talking about policy. The more we try to control, the less control we have."

"You've been reading too many books. Big cities have big issues."

"Maybe. It just seems that the further we go down this road, the more folks tend to resist."

"I think you've got a problem with Chicago."

"No." A CTA bus roared past them. "Well . . . maybe just a little."

"You don't have problems back home in Indiana?"

"Everybody and every place has issues. I just think

Chicago can be a little over the top."

Tony's jaw tightened. "You don't *have* to *live* here. You can always go back to the cornfields."

"I just don't understand a place where there's so little room for open discourse about an overreaching government. What're people so afraid of?"

"Has it ever occurred to you that maybe people *want* the restrictions? That they make us *happy*? Chicago's a *great* place to live. We have Lake Michigan and the Blackhawks. We have Wrigley Field and Rush Street. We have the cleanest, most beautiful city in the country. I think you're jealous."

BERNIE

He sat in the glow of seven computer monitors . . . six of them displaying live video feeds from various locations around the city. On a large center monitor, he focused on the still image of an office — a desk flanked by the Illinois state flag and the U.S. flag. At the corner of the screen, a slightly blurred image of a man appeared in stopped motion next to a desk. Bernie clicked play and watched the image spring to life, the mayor of Chicago walking around his desk, then standing, his back to the camera. Bernie increased the volume then began sawing the barrel of his Mini 14 rifle locked in a vise at his workbench, listening and watching.

Footsteps and shuffling papers echoed through the sound system. *"Well, that went well,"* a man spoke from off-camera. The mayor looked down at his credenza.

"You know," the mayor's nasally voice began, " . . . *when will people move into the Twenty-first Century?"*

"Excuse me, sir?"

The mayor turned, his head still down. He spun a ballpoint pen on his desk. *"They hold onto archaic principles that made sense two-hundred years ago. We've advanced as a society. We don't need a citizen militia anymore."*

"I agree."

"Of course you do, cyborn, I'm the mayor." He smiled and looked up.

They both laughed.

"But, seriously. We have the means to establish perhaps the greatest society since the beginning of time. Without the threat of guns, justice will prevail."

"You're moving in the right direction, sir."

The video feed flickered. Bernie clicked the double bars image on the screen, the word *PAUSE* displaying at the top right hand corner.

It was one of many stored video clips. A motion detector triggered the record function, saving space on the hard drive from which he could retrieve the action segments at his leisure, catalogued by a time stamp.

He'd also developed his own system to track moving objects with a camera mounted on a motorized base. The servo system was expensive, but certain applications were well worth the time and cost to mount them.

Similar systems were commercially available. He'd designed some of them, but he preferred his own improved package, costing much less and avoiding scrutiny from federal agents who closely monitored the surveillance industry.

Bernie selected the Chicago Tribune from his bookmarks. Within minutes, he located and read the short report of the shooting. It said nothing about the casing left in the abandoned apartment building. Surely they'd found it, but for some reason, it wasn't released to the public. "How can a guy start a race war wid out some cooperation?" He sighed.

Another article caught his eye. *"Dying Young in Chicagoland."* Lib Rand had interviewed a psychologist about the increase of drug overdose and suicide in several affluent suburbs, concluding that kids are under too much pressure to succeed.

"Just like parents! Dey climb over each udder, try to geet ahead. Eet's all good. Time to raise stakes."

With his mouse, he exited the Trib and opened a folder, viewing thumbnails, each representing a video file. He sat back, intermittently sawing the barrel of the Mini 14 at his workbench and resting his arm.

"A little *poosh* is all they need. Theen, they geet what dey desarve."

Completing the final strokes with the hack saw, the longer end of the rifle barrel clanged on the concrete floor. Bernie used a small metal file to clean the end of the sawed barrel. The final assembly could wait.

He placed the remaining rifle pieces including the end of the barrel from the floor into a molded foam interior of an open briefcase — closing a latch and sliding the case under his work table.

Sitting in an old office chair, he tapped the keyboard, selecting one of the thumbnails, revealing a still image of a shower room — the top of someone's head appearing at the bottom left corner. He selected *PLAY* with his mouse. Girls' voices echoed on the tiled walls of the room as a blonde girl at the bottom of the screen walked into full view, followed seconds later by a dark haired girl, each adjusting the valves to separate shower heads. Bernie watched the naked girls intently. More voices. Two more girls walked into the shower.

He kicked off his shoes and loosened his belt, realizing he still wore his Atlas Security uniform. He stood, dropping his pants and underwear past his knees before sitting again.

"Bernie!" his mother called from upstairs. "Breakfast ees ready!"

"I'm *Com*eeng!"

LIB

Lib pointed to a large metal sculpture in Daley Plaza. "What *is* that thing?"

"I think it's a baboon. Picasso designed it."

"It's *hid*eous."

"I kinda like it." Tony peered up at the long face of the sculpture. "Mayor Daley wasn't a man of words, but he was quoted in the Tribune on the day of the unveiling. He said, 'We dedicate this celebrated work this morning with the belief that what is strange to us today will be familiar tomorrow.'"

"I can't believe you memorized that line."

"It's part of Chicago lore. I *love* this place."

She knitted her brows. "I'm not a big fan of old man Daley."

Tony's expression revealed his irritation. "Mayor Richard J. Daley had a vision and he saw it through to completion," he said.

They sauntered toward the street, the traffic noise causing them to raise their voices slightly.

"I can see that Chicago is a great city. I'll give you *that* much. But, Daley was a tyrant."

"Some folks don't recognize a good thing when they see it. He knew how to motivate people."

"He knew how to build support with pet projects."

Tony tilted his head and smirked. "That's how the

system works. It's the same in DC."

Lib had shifted her attention to the corner of Washington and Dearborn. "There he is again."

The man in the dark suit stood at the corner. He waved and started toward them.

"Who *is* he?" Lib wondered aloud.

"We'll find out soon enough."

The man, in his late fifties, could have been a former lineman for the Bears, standing six foot six with broad shoulders, his face long and drawn — a little like the sculpture. He looked to either side as though expecting someone else as they drew near. "We need a good place to talk," he said in a deep, monotone voice.

"Why not *here*?" Tony asked.

The man looked around again, then turned back to Tony. "Whatever," he said. "I think I can help you."

"What makes you think we need *help*?"

"I know who you are. I know what you want."

Lib laughed.

Tony cut his eyes at her. She put on a straight face, standing at attention in mock obedience to him.

"Okay, so *prove* it. What do we *want*?"

"You wanna find the shooter."

"You just saw us at the mayor's press conference. A first grader could put that together."

"Your name is Tony Wochowski. You were born at Rush medical center. Your mother died of lung cancer and your father committed suicide."

Tony's expression hardened. "Alright, *ass*hole. That's en*ough*."

"You have no idea what you're getting into."

"What are we getting into?" Lib asked.

"This is much bigger than you think."

"I think we're helping to find a psycho who enjoys shooting innocent people."

The tall stranger looked at Lib, lips drawn together on one side. "So then, why do you think the mayor holds a press conference?"

"He wants to catch the bad guy."

The stranger groaned. "They got no idea who they're dealing with. What you witnessed was an act of desperation. They got nothing. They don't even know if it's a guy."

"Sounds like maybe you *know* who it is." Tony said.

"Well, maybe."

"Why not go there yourself? Why do ya need *us*?"

"My hands are tied, but I know somebody who can help you."

Lib cut her eyes at the stranger. "Why are your hands tied?"

"I don't exist."

Tony and Lib looked at each other. He was dead serious. *Maybe he's an escaped loony*, Lib thought. *Maybe a con artist with an elaborate scam.*

"I know what you're thinking. I'll give you the address and let you find out for yourself."

"I'm not going to any address without knowing who you are and what you want," Tony said.

"My name is Michael. I'm working undercover." He showed no emotion. "I wanna stop a larger plan to undermine our economy and our national security."

"Undercover for who?" Tony asked. The man didn't answer. Tony sighed. "How do we know this isn't a *trap*?"

"I'll go with you to the address. But, this guy won't simply reveal information to you. You gotta find a way to gain his trust. "

"So, how do we gain his *trust*?" Lib asked.

"Not '*we*' but *you*. You can gain his trust."

She felt his eyes on her, sizing her up.

"*Hey*. You've got the *wrong* person." Blood rushed to her face. *He probably wants me to sleep with the guy. Jeez!*

The stranger looked around appearing anxious to leave. "We should forget this whole conversation."

He took two steps toward the Metra station. "Hold *on* a second," Tony called to him. Michael stopped.

Tony turned to Lib. "Let's just hear him out, okay?"

The stranger turned around — his eyebrows furrowed, lips pressed into a thin line —redirecting his attention to Tony. "This guy's special . . . not exactly mister popularity. The broad has a better chance of winning his trust."

The broad! Lib glared at him. *Who is this guy . . . a throwback from the forties*?

Tony shot her another look. *Just calm down*, Lib advised herself. *Don't let your emotions get the best of you.*

The strange man turned back to Lib. "He's a special operative for our government. He has the best available technology at his disposal." Turning his head slightly, he angled his eyes back at her. "You gotta be careful. I'm thinking you should run into him at the corner grocery."

"Sounds like you've already got this planned out," Lib said.

"Actually, yes. But, you need to trust me."

THE GEEK

Lib watched him load six boxes of cereal into his cart. Undoubtedly satisfied by his selection, he marched behind the buggy — multi-colored running shoes plodding flat on the tile floor — an automaton. He was tall and thin, wearing a red and black flannel shirt tucked into oversized blue Dockers tied high around his waist by an equally oversized black belt. The front pocket of his shirt sagged on one side — weighed down by an iPhone with a white cord extending to earbuds planted on each side of his head. He wore a plain black baseball cap with an Apple Computer logo covering a bad haircut pulled down in front.

His name was William Tee. His dossier said he had undergraduate degrees in math and mechanical engineering with a master's in computer science, all from MIT. He'd listed his hobbies as chess and reading. He wasn't married — clearly a permanent condition without divine intervention.

She pushed a cart at a safe distance behind him, waiting for an opportunity.

At the end of the aisle, he abruptly swung 180 degrees and headed back toward Lib. She pushed her buggy into the center of the aisle, pretending to look at cereal, blocking his passage. "Excuse me," he said a little too loud. She looked up at him, prepared to flash her most charming smile . . . *hmmmm* . . . he wasn't looking at her. He looked straight down the aisle.   "Excuse me," he said again without changing his odd gaze. So much for eye contact.

"I'm sorry, but would you mind helping me? You're so tall and I cannot reach the Frosted Flakes."

His gaze swept past her like a lighthouse beacon, responding to her request. "Frosted Flakes are very high in sugar and carbohydrates," he said, reaching up then handing her the box. He looked at her for a moment but looked back at his cart a split second later.

She patted the top of his hand. "Thank you," she said. "You're very kind."

"I need more cereal," he announced, looking again down the aisle.

"Oh, I'm sorry." She moved aside, allowing him to pass.

It wouldn't be easy.

She walked several feet, then paused, waiting to see which direction he'd go.   He grabbed two more boxes, guided his cart to the end of the aisle and disappeared to the left. Making her way around the corner and following his movement from the opposite end of the store, she saw him wheel his way into the beverage aisle. She entered the aisle from the other end, pretending not to notice, moving her buggy in his direction. He abruptly turned and went back in the direction from which he'd entered. Launch Plan B.

She'd noticed a bicycle helmet in his cart. She paid for her cereal and walked outside, spotting a bicycle chained to one of the brick columns in front of the store near a picnic table. She sat down and waited.

Lib thought about her Aunt Maggie with cancer. Nope. She never really liked Aunt Maggie anyway. She thought about her friend in high school, paralyzed in an automobile accident, the saddest moment of her young life. Lib spent days with her, trying to cheer her up. Then, her friend had taken a bottle of pain pills, committing suicide. Lib began to cry.

Bill exited the store and loaded one plastic bag into a basket in front and two bags into additional baskets mounted like saddlebags on both sides of the rear wheel. He strapped on a helmet fitted with two small rearview mirrors, wedging his cap into the front basket. He paused for a moment, seeming unsure of which direction to go.

"Why are you crying?" he asked. It wasn't exactly an empathetic tone. He was genuinely puzzled.

"I'm new to the area. I don't know anybody," she sniffed. "I unpacked my computer and it doesn't work."

"I know a lot about computers," he said.

"Would you please help me?"

He stood for a moment. It was awkward, but Lib took the risk that Plan B would work. She waited. *What is he thinking? How long does it take a guy to catch on? One Mississippi, two Mississippi . . .*

"Where do you live?"

"I live in Apartment 12 B, Twin Lakes Apartment Complex, five blocks from here."

"That's where I live."

"What a coincidence," she said.

* * *

The apartment she'd rented that afternoon was empty except for a computer on the floor of the living room and an air mattress in the bedroom, just in case she needed a few days. She waited for him to arrive on his bicycle.

She heard footsteps. A mechanical bell clanking the arrival of her guest, she peered at the large image of his alien helmet through the sight glass, waiting a few seconds before opening the door. "C'mon in."

"You look . . . a little different," Bill stated bluntly, looking directly past her at the bare walls.

She wore pink lipstick and she'd unbuttoned the top button of her blouse. *Wow. Talk about clueless.*

"Here's my computer." She leaned over the PC lying on the carpet of the living room area, her blouse hanging open just a little.

He checked the plug. He turned on the unit. Nothing. He switched the plug to the other outlet. Nothing.

"It's probably the power supply. Let me check one more thing."

Standing and flipping the switch near the door, the computer monitor blinked and the hard drive whirred.

"You have a switched power outlet for a lamp. It was not on."

"I'm so embarrassed. I'm just not good with electronics at all."

"I work with computers."

Lib smiled. "Would you like something to drink?"

"No." He stood for a moment, still wearing the helmet with two antennae. A puzzled look crossed his face. "You don't have furniture."

"Not yet. I'm just getting started. I have the computer and an air mattress . . . that's about it."

"Oh."

They stood in silence for fifteen seconds. Though uncomfortable with dead air space in general, she waited, hoping to put him at ease with less chatter.

"I would like a glass of water," he said.

"Okay." She waited a split second longer. *Just look at me, dammit! One Mississippi, two Mississippi . . .* He looked at her, no doubt wondering why it took her so long to retrieve his drink. She smiled at him the same way she'd smiled at Bobby Claxton in the first grade. He looked down, revealing an almost imperceptible smile. "I'll be right back," she said, lightly touching his hand with her fingers.

THE MAYOR

"Mr. Mayor, Smitty's here to see you."

"Send 'im in."

The mayor stared at the portraits of his predecessors. Carter Harrison, Sr. and Anton Cermak were both assassinated in office. Richard J. Daley and Harold Washington also died in office. Occupational hazards, he thought and smiled. Better than being governor, since most of them were serving time.

"Good morning Smitty."

"Mornin' Jay."

"I need a favor," Mayor Epstein said.

Smitty never visited unless there was a favor involved on either side.

The mayor removed his glasses and pinched the bridge of his nose. "I need support for a new gun law."

Smitty said nothing. He waited.

"We need to convince the other Aldermen to pass a ban on guns."

Smitty shifted his weight. "Sir, you mean automatic weapons don't you?"

"No. I mean guns. All of them. I'm tired of waking up every morning and reading about some baby wounded or killed by a stray bullet."

"You'll get resistance.

"Oy *vay*! I know. But, I think we now have public support."

"What about the AG?

"What about him?"

"He'll annoy the *hell* out of you."

Jay Epstein laughed. "Pat Thompson annoys the hell out of me without saying a word."

Smitty chuckled. "I'll make a few calls. We'll call a special session."

Smitty leaned forward in his chair, ready to stand.

The mayor held up his hand to stop him. "Not so fast. There's something else."

Smitty sat back in the chair as the mayor lifted a file from his desk.

"John Amos is on his way over," the mayor said.

"You meet with the police chief several times a week. What's special about today?"

"I wanna investigate these folks."

The mayor slid the file folder across the desk to Smitty. Smitty lifted the folder and thumbed through pages of names and addresses.

"Who're these people?"

"They're all batshit crazy. I wanna know what they're doing and who they're doing it with."

"The ACLU won't like it."

"I don't give a damn about the ACLU. I wanna know what these folks are up to."

The phone buzzed. "Mr. Mayor?"

"Yes, Doris."

"The AG is on line four."

"Tell 'im I'm busy."

"He said it's important."

"*You* know the drill, Doris. Do your damn *job*!"

The mayor shook his head in disgust. "Okay Smitty. Let's show this country how it's done."

BERNIE

Smitty stood . . . the image on the screen froze with Smitty extending his hand to the Mayor, *PAUSE* displaying at the top right hand corner of the screen.

Bernie shifted his attention away from the still image of the mayor's office to a small machine attached to his desktop, resembling a small turret of a tank with a short barrel pointed at the opposite wall. A cell phone with a makeshift terminal strip sat nearby, wires connecting to small servo motors on the turret.

The device was temporarily anchored to the desk with wood screws. He tapped a few keys on his keyboard and the opposite wall of the basement appeared on the screen. With a joystick, he moved the turret from side to side, watching the shifting image. The camera and the servo controls worked well. Overall, it weighed four pounds, most of the weight from the short sawed off barrel of a Mini 14. He pushed a button and a red dot appeared on the basement wall. Again, he moved the turret from side to side, watching the dot move along the wall. He raised and lowered the barrel with the remote device. The dot moved up and down. *So far, so good*.

He directed the dot at a steel box on the floor, stuffed with an old quilt his mother made for him as a child. Bernie put on headphones before lifting a black plastic cover on the controls revealing a green button, taking a deep breath. He looked at the screen and adjusted the turret until the red dot covered an intersection of two geometric lines on the quilt. Pressing the button, he heard a muffled pop and the sound of the steel box sliding several inches on the concrete floor. A wisp of smoke escaped through a small hole at the intersection of lines on the quilt. It worked.

Bernie stood and flipped a light switch. Several fluorescent bulbs flickered before illuminating a machine shop on the longer wall of the basement with a lathe, drill press and an end mill, older models purchased during the liquidation of a local tool and die business that had filed for bankruptcy.

At the far end of the organized benches, an oblong helium filled balloon floated beneath the floor joists. Bernie inspected several small fans on each side of the balloon. He moved a five position selector switch on the controls still in his hand and slid a lever forward to power the fans. He then used the joy stick to adjust the angle of the fans, also mounted on servo-controlled bases. The balloon strained against the tension of the cords, trying to break free.

With his free hand, he put a small s-hook through one of several eyelet flaps on the bottom of the tethered balloon. Stepping toward another work bench, he placed a small tray on a scale and loaded four pounds of lead shot before turning and attaching it to the s-hook. He reduced the speed of the fans and the balloon settled a little, finding equilibrium above its mooring. It was enough buoyancy to hold the balloon, the fans, and the small turret.

"You peek into *my* life, steal from me. Now, I peek eento *your* lives, and steal it *back*, you, rrred *bool*!"

Bernie felt his heart beating a primordial rhythm as he slid his foot forward on the concrete floor. His hips followed his foot as he snapped and popped his body into consecutive poses, like a matador stepping into the ring. He stepped and stopped, turned and paused. He heard trumpets playing a victory song.

He was the man! He was on fire! He would demonstrate his prowess to Chicago, the city that laid him low, slapping his face again and again. He was now ready.

Bernie, the matador, marched back to his bench — tilting his shoulders one way, then another as he stomped — chest out — advancing and pausing, advancing and pausing — head turned to one side, dragging one foot behind each step. He was the great bullfighter in the ring with the red Chicago Bull — snorting fire and kicking dirt.

He saw the chat icon on his screen with a number two. He resumed his position in front of the main screen, reading two postings from Jack, his mentor, his encourager.

"Stay focused, Bernie. I need you," read the first through encryption software.

"Make sure your generator is working, you may lose power," read the second.

Bernie tapped his reply back. "Test results positive." He encrypted the note and sent it. Bernie followed with a second message. "When?"

He waited a moment. A familiar "doodle link" sound signaled the reply.

"Soon."

LIB

Bill had left her apartment with more of a spring in his step — poor thing. Maybe he'd find someone one day. Lib didn't want to get too close. She knew the consequences. For someone like Bill, it could be extremely difficult. She'd be a friend to him — maybe build his confidence a little.

She'd known a few guys like Bill in college. They were insecure and clingy.

Bill reminded her how much she appreciated Tony with his tough guy persona and his confidence. Sadly, Tony seemed inattentive and selfish. Why couldn't she assemble the perfect mate from spare parts? She could build him from the ground up to meet her exact specifications. She thought she'd found one guy in grad school but he turned out to be a jerk. Besides, if Tony had any really good qualities, he'd be married. Her mom warned her about single guys in their thirties.

He'd taken her around Chicago that first year, offering her a taste of her new surroundings, expecting her to fall into the Chicago way. Chicago — the city of broad shoulders — was unique, he'd said. Most cities are feminine. Not Chicago. Chicago's a he, tough and proud of his industrial heritage. Perhaps no place on earth has a greater sense of regional pride. Not New York. Not even Dallas. Chicagoans love their city and they'll fight anyone who disparages it. Despite his efforts, Lib had maintained her objectivity, even among the most rabid defenders of Chicago culture. To her, it was just another large city.

Lib's early work had bordered on muck raking journalism. She'd asked questions that Chicagoans don't ask. She'd already caused controversy for the Trib. Jones — the Metro Editor — spent most of his time counseling her, helping her to understand the political landscape and the people. Yet, she'd asked the tough questions. *Shouldn't somebody?*

The dashboard clock in her car showed ten minutes past eight. *Tony doesn't like to wait.*

She pulled into Starbucks, parking her Jeep next to Tony's Camaro. He sat near the window facing out — glaring at her as she waved on her way through the door.

"Where've you *been*?"

"I'm sorry. I ran late."

He smirked. "You can buy me a double expresso for my trouble."

"Okay."

She placed an order and listened to the shushing sound as the barista steamed milk for the latte in front of her. She ordered regular coffee with hazelnut and a double shot for Tony who used a finger to manipulate his phone.

Peering over her shoulder, Lib surveyed the morning crowd. One woman laughed, staring at a tablet. Everyone was on an electronic device, sending e-mails and texting each other. Couples sat at the same table, each oblivious to the other. Absurd.

She collected the drinks with her purse hung over one arm and worked her way back to the table at the window.

"Here's your double expresso."

He sipped his drink. "So, what's he like?"

She thought about Bill for a second, not wanting to

characterize him unfairly. "He's nice."

"That's it? You're a journalist for God's sake! What kinda answer is that?"

Tony seemed unusually irritable.

"He's different, just like the man said. But, I think maybe he's just hypersensitive."

"Well, I'm sure you'll find a way to get him out of his shell."

"What's that supposed to mean?"

"I'm sure you can warm him up."

Lib shook her head. They'd worked together for almost a year. He'd never spoken this way before. *What's going on in that big, fat head? Is he jealous?* "Maybe I can," she said. "That's the whole point."

"Well, don't be surprised if junior falls hard."

It wasn't Tony's style to show any signs of interest in another person's feelings.

He sipped his coffee, showing little emotion.

"Don't worry," she assured him. "I have a backup plan."

"You know he'll fall in love with you if you sleep with him."

"I have no intention of sleeping with him. But, it's really none of your *bus*iness now, *is* it?"

She saw a slight tinge around his eyes. *Was he hurt by my comment?* It wasn't her intent to hurt him, it just came out funny.

"That's right. Do whatever you want."

Clearly, Tony felt more than he'd let on.

The barista steamed milk for another customer.

She tried to think of something to say. Anything to cut through the awkward silence. "I invited him to dinner for helping me with my computer."

"Maybe you should serve a bottle of wine."

"Actually, that's a good idea. Maybe it'll loosen things up a little."

"Based on what I read, you may need a few Vicodin to loosen *that* nut."

"He's not a nut. He's just an introvert."

"Well, give me a call if you need backup."

He looked at her. She'd never really noticed the unusual blueness of his eyes before. Maybe he was more attentive than she'd believed. Maybe he could actually be a decent guy.

"*Buuuurrrrrrpppppp!*"

Or, maybe not.

TOM AND GEORGE

The two men sat facing an old, coffee stained metal console amid three banks of video monitors — eight monitors mounted on a center panel and four mounted on panels angled to either side. Each monitor alternated images of stores, hotel lobbies, jewelry stores and parking lots. The main screen displayed an image of Lib and Tony from a camera mounted high above them.

Tom pushed his cap back, a tuft of iron gray, curly hair on top of his head now visible in the light from the monitors. George took a bite from half a donut.

Tom said, "These two don't seem capable."

"Give 'em a chance. Michael's there to assist."

George sighed.

Tom fished money from his pocket, a one and a two dollar bill, laying them side by side on the console. "You know, Georgie, I wonder what they were thinkin' when they designed these bills?"

"What do you mean?"

"Am I two times more important?"

George shook his head. "Nah. It means I'm number one. You, sir, are out of circulation."

THE GEEK

He couldn't stop thinking about her. *What a distraction!* She'd asked him over for dinner. What would he wear? What would they *talk* about? He wasn't good at conversation. Strike that. He wasn't good at normal conversation. He could talk for hours about matrices and protocols. He understood math and physics and engineering intuitively. He didn't know the first thing about ordinary people. They talked about things of little interest to him. He just never understood how most common folks could go on for hours without saying *anything* of substance.

What if she wanted to have sex? He was okay with that. He'd studied it. He knew all the terminology. He had a drawer full of condoms — just in case.

There had been a few close calls. He'd knocked over a lamp and ruined the mood for one study partner at MIT. The falling floor lamp wouldn't have been so bad, but it hit the poor girl in the mouth — breaking two of her front teeth and bloodying her lip. Then he committed the ultimate faux pas. He had told her that she looked like a hillbilly camel with her swollen upper lip and broken teeth. *What was the girl's name? Sandra. Sandra the Saharan hillbilly camel.* He laughed at the image in his mind.

What is her name? Lib. I shouldn't forget her name. What is it short for? It didn't matter. She was the most beautiful girl he'd ever met. Why would she take an interest in him? Where would they sit to eat their dinner? Maybe on the air mattress. That would be awkward. *What will she cook?*

He paced around his apartment. He had to calm down, or it would be a disaster. He sat in a chair. *Okay, okay. Just breathe. That's it. Take a few deep breathes.* It would all be over in a few hours. He'd do or say something she wouldn't understand and that would be the end of it. *No big deal. Just breathe.*

He thought about his friend in elementary school. Debbie. She had understood him. She didn't care that the other kids teased him. They played chess together. She was smart and she was pretty. Maybe Lib was like Debbie. Maybe she played chess. *Okay, okay. Don't build it up, Bill. Just breathe.*

He started to feel a little better. He knew that he overanalyzed everything. He also knew that it never worked out when he tried to analyze people. *Just leave it alone. Don't go there! Try to relax.* He started to relax but, he wasn't in her apartment so it didn't matter. *Okay, overanalyzing again.* Maybe he could buy some beer or something. He hated beer. What about wine? He could have a glass of wine. He had a bottle of cooking wine in his cabinet, a gift from his mother. He'd have a glass or two before going to her apartment.

How does a girl like Lib end up with an empty apartment? It didn't make sense to him. *Okay, stop thinking so much. Just accept it and move on. Maybe I should do a little work. Maybe that will help settle me down.*

Bill walked into the spare bedroom converted to an office. He loved the tiny red and green lights from his computer equipment glowing in the darkness of the room before turning on the light. It gave him a sense of value. He understood the machines and they responded to his commands. It was his comfort zone among machines who never judged him. They were there for him. If something malfunctioned, he cared for them.

He sat in an office chair and typed in several passwords. The screen responded to his rapid typing, a skill developed during two years of typing in high school to escape the humiliation of PE. He'd also liked being around the girls.

He read a few postings on a special website that he'd developed. Sent messages encrypted and received messages decoded by software, also developed by him. The messages to and from headquarters, keeping him apprised of his regular assignments. He clicked on the last message received.

"Monitoring chatter hourly. Need to maintain remote access to their computers until we make our move. Keep me informed."

Bill's special encryption software also provided NSA with the means to decode other messages. His current assignment was to locate and monitor several suspects in the Chicago area. Bill had driven around for hours collecting WIFI signals. It was surprisingly easy to run a quick routine — attempting millions of password combinations until getting through — though it was time consuming and Chicago is a big city.

The IP addresses constantly changed. The suspects had developed a system, moving around and setting up decoys, making it almost impossible to keep track. Bill had cracked their system. He knew a few of their locations which he'd pinned on a detailed map of Chicago.

Monitoring chatter was important. But, it was equally important to maintain a safe distance. The information was more important than apprehending the bad guys who would provide more value to the NSA as informants. Of course, the suspects sometimes sent messages intended to create a diversion — perhaps suspicious they were being monitored at some point — further emphasizing the need for stealth.

Bill read a few of many decoded messages — hay in the haystack. He looked for the needle. Something caught his eye. *You may lose power*. It was ominous, but it was also verifiable — albeit after the fact. If they lose power, they know they have their man.

Bill entered copious notes from which common threads could be assembled from the otherwise random information. It was a special process that Bill had developed.

He reminded himself of his value. It kept him going. He didn't have time for socializing. Besides, there would be time to enjoy life one day.

He already had a comfortable retirement at 33. His cloaking technology was his crowning achievement. It would protect soldiers, but it wasn't all about recognition. Besides, he couldn't receive recognition. It was top secret.

For Bill, it was not that complex. He had simply created a substrate that would reflect images in perfect light and proportion to what existed on the other side. They were pleased with his development, but he had no idea of the importance at first. He'd become a protected asset, receiving compensation for his contribution in an account delayed until long after the technology was deployed. Until then, he had a responsibility to keep the information to himself.

Some days, he wanted the recognition — particularly when teased in public. He wanted people to know of his contribution to his country. But, he also understood sacrifice. His grandfather had served in World War II, part of a different generation of people who answered the call without question. It was duty. Bill's father had served in Vietnam. Bill loved his father. He hoped his father was proud, watching from heaven.

Bill looked at his watch. *Oh my God*! Almost time. He walked into the bathroom, looking at himself in the mirror. He opened a cabinet and retrieved an electric trimmer.

MAYOR

"Chuck Woolsey is on line one, sir." The mayor recognized the name — an actor who played mostly military roles in Hollywood — a conservative and the new President of the NRA.

The mayor picked up the phone. "Mr. Woolsey. I *thought* you might call." The mayor spun to one side in his chair, appearing deep in thought. He responded to the phone. "No need for that kind of language. I respect your work. But, we have a situation here."

Holding the phone away from his ear, Epstein made a face.

"Hello?"

He pressed a button on his desk. "*Doris*! Have somebody send some flowers to the Waldorf Astoria for Chuck Woolsey. He's arriving this afternoon."

"Schmuck," the mayor muttered.

He sat slumped in his chair for a moment, his partially laced fingers cradling his chin. He pressed the button again.

"*Doris*! Call Tony Wochowski at the *Trib* and somebody at WGN. I wanna meet Woolsey at the hotel and I want some *cameras* there!"

BERNIE

The image froze on the screen.

Bernie tapped a message. "*NRA President arriving in hours. Mayor meeting at Waldorf Astoria.*" He encrypted the message and sent it.

A few moments later, a reply message appeared.

"*Do it.*"

Bernie pulled up Google Maps and typed in his home address and the address for the Waldorf Astoria, Chicago. He received directions on the screen and a map with a blue line showing the best route. It wasn't that far away. He looked at a photo image at street level. It had a courtyard. *Nice place*.

He checked the weather forecast. *Winds out of the Northwest at 5 mph*. Tricky, but he'd manage.

TONY

Tony's phone beeped — a text message from his editor. *The mayor wants you to meet him at Waldorf Astoria.*

Tony dialed the office. "What's up?"

"The mayor's setting up a photo op with the President of the NRA. He wants you there."

"That's interesting. Those two don't belong on the same *planet*, much less in the same *room* together."

"It's a favor. I think we might be smart to take advantage of it."

"Right."

Tony hung up the phone and put it in his pocket. He didn't mind. It was not that far away, but he needed to clean up a bit.

He thought about Lib, probably dolled up for the geek. He shook his head. He'd really said too much to her. Now, there'd be tension between 'em.

Maybe it'd be better if he spelled it out to her. He wanted her. He wanted her in the kitchen and the bathroom and the elevator — raw desires. But this was different. He wanted to wake up next to her. He wanted to spend Christmas with her. Lib was everything he wanted.

Tony tried to shake it off. It wasn't his style. He'd felt this way once before — a disaster. He ended up looking like a fool. He'd since found comfort in his boorish manner. It was easier that way. No mess.

His friends had fallen into the same trap. One minute, they were regular guys — going to Bears' games and talking too loud at bars. The next minute, they're carrying shopping bags at Marshall Field's, commenting on clothing, pretending to care. His best friend Roger was the latest casualty. Tony tried to save him. It was no use. Roger was now among the walking dead. He couldn't hang out anymore — fearful of spraining his uterus.

LIB

Okay. Lasagna's in the oven. Wine's in the fridge. Plastic utensils. Check. Paper plates. Check. Plastic wine goblets. Check. Napkins. Check.

Lib examined herself in the bathroom mirror. She would soon have crow's feet around her eyes like her mother. For the moment, she'd try not to think about it. Aging was inevitable.

She decided against makeup. Bill seemed like the kind of guy who might appreciate more of a natural look. She put on her non-prescription glasses and held a hair clip in her mouth as she pulled her hair back.

What would she talk about? Having conversation with Bill wasn't easy. Maybe she needed to give him space — room to breathe. It really wasn't natural for her. She was a talker and full of opinions. This would not be the full-on engagement that she sought among her colleagues. It was mock innocence, a role she despised. She wasn't a wall flower.

Extraordinary circumstances sometimes require extraordinary measures. She'd try to relax and let him talk when he felt like talking. How she hated dead air space! Ordinarily, she'd say something just to break an awkward pause in the conversation. Somehow, she had to control it. She had to maintain her composure and put on a sweet face for this poor, unfortunate creature.

Lib walked into the kitchen and retrieved a cheap corkscrew, one of only a few utensils in a drawer next to the fridge. She removed a clear plastic goblet from a cellophane wrapper and examined it. *Pitiful.* She opened a bottle of wine and poured much closer to the rim than usual. Maybe it would help.

The doorbell rang. *Shit!* She gulped the wine and rinsed the goblet before walking to the door.

She peered at the fisheye image of Bill standing with something in his hand. *What is it? Oh God! Maybe he's going to kill me! Or worse, maybe he's planning to rape me. Focus, Lib.*

She opened the door with a smile. He looked past her — a slight improvement over looking away. "C'mon in."

He stepped through the door holding a wrapped package. Closing the door behind him, she waited. *One Mississippi, two Mississippi . . . Nothing.* She wanted to ask him what he had in his hand to help get him back on track. It was gonna be a long night.

"Oh." He seemed to wake up from a coma. "I brought you some chocolates." He handed the package to her wrapped in children's birthday paper.

"Oh, *thank* you." *Why do you wrap a gift and then tell someone what's in it?*

She walked into the kitchen area and put the box on the counter.

"Open it."

"Oh, *I'm* sorry." She opened the box. It wasn't just any chocolates. It was Leonidas Belgian chocolates — her favorite. She stood looking at the elaborate tin before realizing that she was now the one who looked silly. *How did he know? Was it coincidence?* Ordinarily, she'd drill quickly through his skull to collect answers to her questions.

Bill fidgeted.

Lib snapped out of her momentary stupor. "I made lasagna." *One Mississippi, two Mississippi.* "Would you like some wine?"

"Okay."

That's it? she thought. *Okay?*

She edged around him, her breasts unintentionally brushing against his arm. "All I have is white wine. I hope that's okay."

"Okay."

She poured two plastic goblets, returning the bottle to the fridge before raising her glass. He'd already finished. "Salute!" She said, draining her glass like a shot of bad tequila.

BERNIE

A limo emerged from below the camera's view. It turned slowly through an elaborate stone gate into a courtyard with a fountain in the center. The brochure said it was voted the number one hotel in the Continental U.S. *Nice.*

Bernie could see other limos and a few black Lincolns parked around the circular drive. Men in dark suits and sunglasses stood at various locations, the mayor waiting near the door.

Bernie made a few adjustments and flipped a switch. The angle of the mayor improved on the screen, his head now slightly below center. Bernie flipped another switch and pressed a button. He could see it on the stonework above the door. A small red dot. He pressed the button again and it disappeared.

Bernie flipped the function switch and zoomed out. The limo moved slowly into view again — stopping in front of the double doors. The mayor and the limo were both in the bottom portion of the screen. Bernie used the joy stick to adjust the image, centering the mayor's head. Bernie zoomed in again, the back of someone's head appearing from the side. The man turned — the NRA President. Bernie's fingers trembled as he flipped the switch and pressed a button. He couldn't see the red dot. He frantically moved the joystick, now controlling the turret with laser scope. The dot appeared on the mayor's shoulder. Bernie knew he only had a few seconds. He raised the dot, then to the left. He lifted the cover and pressed the green button.

Bernie watched Chuck Woolsey slump to the ground and the mayor leaning over him. He flipped the switch, using the joystick to maneuver his device. Buildings appeared on the monitor, then trees that lined the street. He made his way east, using the remaining charge to relocate his hovering drone where the battery could recharge in direct sunlight.

Within minutes, Bernie saw open blue sky. He allowed the blimp to drift eastward in the wind, gaining a new charge, moving far beyond the shoreline above Lake Michigan. He would retrieve it later.

It was done. He'd done it. Moving to his workstation, he tapped a few keys, displaying a live feed from CNN. They reported the incident. Adjusting the volume, he listened to Wolf Blitzer describe the scene outside the hotel. Bernie sat back — basking in the glow from the monitor.

Blitzer described the growing tension between the mayor and the NRA. He recounted the recent shootings and reported a chronology of events leading up to the proposed ban. "*Now this. The NRA President shot in Chicago. We'll continue to monitor the situation and keep you apprised of further developments.*"

The scene replayed again and again. Bernie couldn't get enough.

The television camera had picked up someone standing near the doorway. Bernie leaned forward and captured the still image. He blew it up on the screen. It was Tony Wochowski, investigative reporter at the *Trib*.

TONY

Tony ran to his car parked illegally in the street. There he'd sit with his laptop, feverishly typing the jumbled thoughts and images, still fresh in his mind.

He'd heard a bang. It came from above, near the street. There were buildings in that direction, mostly obscured by trees. He felt the terror of standing in view of a sniper — maybe perched in the trees across the road. He'd seen something moving, like a large piece of newspaper, floating slowly, unusually high above the street. It had disappeared around the corner.

He'd seen the glistening blood stain under Woolsey's head growing larger — seeking gaps between the stones on the walk in front of the hotel before the scene was overrun by security. *How could it happen? Who would've known? It was an impromptu visit. Maybe the mayor was the target.*

Tony felt a pang of guilt. He was terrified, but also excited. This was his work — what moved him out of bed in the mornings. He thrived on it, yet, he'd never witnessed anything this horrific. Woolsey was dead. There was little doubt.

Tony couldn't forget the odd split second image — Woolsey's head partially buried in the concrete like a mask had been dropped on the walkway. The back of his head was gone! His eyes were still open, but they were different — sunken and dull and still, a red hole and a small amount of blood between them. His skin also looked different — gray and lifeless. The man was dead before his body hit the ground.

What about his family? Did he have kids?

Tony typed everything like a free association exercise in creative writing — his stream of consciousness capturing every thought — every image. He'd witnessed something evil, something dark and disturbing. *What would be the fallout from this event? The NRA President killed in Chicago next to the mayor. What if this were an al Qaeda plot?* Liberals and conservatives were already on the brink of violence. *What will happen now?*

With a dry, hollow ache in his stomach, he recalled September 11th, 2001 — a feeling that everything had changed in the world. It was nausea, but it was more — a longing for what existed just hours before. Tony wanted a simple existence. At the moment, he didn't understand the place that was his home. It no longer made sense. Perhaps he'd witnessed a cataclysmic event. Perhaps this ushered in a new era. 9-11 resulted in The Patriot Act, paving the way for a more aggressive approach to terrorism. What could be the fallout from this event? He imagined liberals calling for more gun controls — for martial law. It was unsettling. Similarly, he could predict the posture of the conservatives. They would warn us about an overreaching government, while reacting with yet more laws. It was a paradox. They'd claim to err on the side of liberty, urging lawmakers and the American people to resist the immediate desire for protection, yet, like the Patriot Act, such rhetoric would give way to overly invasive policies.

TOM AND GEORGE

George watched Wolf Blitzer on one of the monitors. "Were we wrong, Tom?"

Tom sighed. "I don't think so, Georgie. This isn't about law abiding citizens.   It's about enemies of the state. Terrorists."

"But what happens when terrorists are citizens?"

"It's not the *guns*, I tell you.   It's a criminal element that's out of control. Taking guns away from the good guys is not a good solution."

George shook his head. "I can't believe it's come to this. We gave them every opportunity and it's slipping away."

Tom inspected his fingernails. "Wonder what they think about us, now?"

"What do you mean?" George asked.

"I wonder what most Americans think of our work as founding fathers."

"I think they *like* us, Tom.   Our names are on *every*thing."

"I'm not so sure anymore.   Maybe they'd think *we're* extremists."

BERNIE

Bernie watched the live feed of the mayor's office. Ordinarily, he'd let the algorithm do its work, allowing the action to unfold and watching the recorded video after the fact. He couldn't wait. He wanted to see the mayor, even if it meant watching an empty room on a screen for hours.

It wasn't long before he heard voices. He heard the mayor, barely audible, perhaps in the hallway shouting, but he couldn't make out the words.

The mayor walked into view and stood behind his desk.

Bernie heard another voice, recognizing the police chief, John Amos.

"Mr. Mayor, we were there. I had men all around the area."

"You missed something."

"We immediately shut down the streets for blocks. Nobody could have gotten out without our notice."

"What about the buildings across the street?" the mayor asked.

"We've been through them. Not a trace. Nothing."

"You've missed something," he said again.

"I've got guys who're still questioning anyone and everyone in the area."

"I wanna know everything as soon as you find out. I want you to pick up every known nutcase in the city. I don't care about the ACLU. Just gather 'em up," Epstein said.

The mayor picked up a glass paperweight from his desk and tossed it in his hand a few times like a pitcher on the mound with a resin bag. He drew back and hurled the paperweight wildly across the room, followed immediately by a crash and the sound of tinkling glass.

"*Sir*?!"

"*Get out*! *Get out of my office*!"

A door slammed. The mayor plopped down in his chair, then leaned over his desk with his face in his hands.

BILL

Bill held his fourth glass of wine. They sat on the carpeted floor of the living room near the sliding glass doors, a darkening view of a parking lot and the sun setting over the shadowy silhouette of several tall buildings. Two paper plates stained with residual tomato and cheese sat nearby — receptacles for wadded napkins and plastic forks. One empty wine bottle and a second half bottle were both corked, laying down between them.

She hugged her knees — her face glowing in the last sliver of orange sunlight peeking over the buildings.

He couldn't believe how comfortable he felt. She wasn't anything like his first impression of her. She seemed relaxed and unpretentious — enjoying the quiet exchange of dinner talk. Now, they sat with little need to impress one another. He liked that. She shifted position, leaning back on her back-stretched arms for support. He could see the shape of her breasts through her sweater. She crossed her legs. Something stirred inside of him. He wanted to kiss her, but wouldn't risk interrupting the moment. It wasn't everyday that a beautiful woman invited him to dinner. Actually, a beautiful woman had never invited him to dinner.

She gazed through the window. "Ever wonder what's going on out there in all those buildings?"

"Not really."

"I guess I wonder about the individual lives of so many

people. We have no idea about their pain, joy, and anger."

He thought for a second. It was true. He'd never really given it much thought. "I think most of them are the same. They start out trying to fulfill a dream and at some point, it becomes drudgery."

"I don't want to live like *that*, do *you*?"

She looked at him. He felt oddly comfortable looking directly at her. He knew he had a habit of looking anywhere but the eyes.

"No," he said. "I want a quiet, peaceful life." He paused a moment, then added, "I think ambition is way overrated."

She smiled. "Maybe you're right. But, wouldn't it be nice if you could do something to change the world?"

Maybe he had done something to change the world. He looked at her, wondering if he could trust her, wanting her to like him. He wanted to tell her about his inventions.

She sat up. "Wait right here. I have something to show you." She stood and walked a few steps toward the hallway, then abruptly turned and walked back to him. She leaned down and kissed his cheek, then walked back to the bedroom.

His heart pounded in his chest. *"Can this be real?"* He suppressed the urge to jump up and pace the floor.

A few minutes later, she came back into the room holding her purse and a small photo book. She flipped on the light and sat next to him on the floor. "This is my family," she said, handing him the leather bound case.

He unsnapped the flap and opened it. The first photos were yellowed with age. They were photos of her as a little girl. In one photo, she sat on her father's lap, perched on a large farm tractor.

"That's my dad."

She turned the page. "Here I am in the third grade." Bill looked at a photo of eight year old Lib, missing a tooth in front.

Their thighs were touching. Her face was close. He turned and kissed the side of her mouth. She smiled, but continued sharing the photos of a birthday, her graduation from high school, her graduation from college, and a picture of Lib with a black and white Shih Tzu.

He pointed. "Who is that?"

"Oh, that's Rufus. He was my best friend in the whole world," her voice cracking a little.

"I understand. I have a two year old Cocker Spaniel. His name is Rex."

She sniffed. He put his arm around her. He wanted more, but he also wanted to avoid the mistakes of his past. He had allowed his emotions to get the best of him before and had advanced too quickly. The results were in. He had freaked them out and had never gotten past second base. This time, he kept his cool — pacing his moves.

Lib was different. She didn't get up and leave when he kissed her. She stayed next to him, thighs touching. She trusted him. Maybe he should trust her. Maybe he should tell her a little bit about himself. He swallowed hard.

"I'm an inventor."

"Really? What *kind* of inventor?"

"I invented a cloaking device that is being used by the military."

"I've heard of something like that." She appeared comfortable, approachable.

"It can be worn like a poncho, allowing soldiers to walk undetected in broad daylight."

"*Wow*! Are you *ser*ious?"

"Yes. I am serious. But, it is top secret."

"Okay," she smiled. "You had me *going* there for a minute. Now, I think you're pulling my *leg*."

"No. I can show it to you. But, you must promise not to tell anyone."

"If you ask me not to tell anyone, I won't tell anyone."

The light flickered, then darkness surrounded them. Outside, a slight glow to the west outlined the tops of the buildings dotted with only a few emergency lights.

"I think we lost power," he said.

"You're amazing," her voice answered in the dark.

TONY

Tony listened to Lib's voicemail greeting as he drove on Clark Street, lit only by headlights from cars. *"Lib, call me. It's important."*

It wasn't his style to leave more than one message. This was an exception. Something felt very wrong. He thought about the strange man at Daley Plaza. *What was his name? Michael.* He thought about the geek and Lib. He thought about the image of Woolsey lying on the ground in a pool of blood. Suddenly, he was suspicious of everything — the same feelings he experienced in '01.

He wanted to go to Lib's makeshift apartment, but quickly ruled it out. He needed a drink. Ahead, the bluish glow from an emergency light inside of a convenience store drew his attention. Parking his car in front of the store, he sat wondering about the power outage before lifting himself from the seat and approaching the door, pulling it. Locked. A woman waved him away from inside — a look of panic in her expression. She motioned again, this time mouthing "Power's out. Come back later."

By the time Tony arrived home, a single light glowed from inside the efficiency apartment. Power had not been lost or had been restored. The old metal stairs groaned as he made his way to the door, unlocking both deadbolt locks. The shade was partially up. The shade on his door was always down. *Strange.*

Tony stepped inside his apartment, looking around. A fluorescent light underneath the cabinet in the adjoining kitchen allowed him to survey the room before switching on the overhead. The .38 revolver sat on the dresser where he'd left it. *If someone had been inside, they would've taken it.* He felt relieved.

Tony stuffed the revolver in the back of his pants. Leaning over the bed, he grabbed the remote and clicked on the television in the corner of the room and watched CNN's coverage of the shooting. Nothing new. Woolsey had been pronounced dead. He was divorced with two adult children and a young grandson. They ran an interview with the mayor from just minutes earlier.

"This is a cowardly act." Epstein stopped for a moment to regain his composure. He looked directly at the camera and pointed his finger. *"I want to deliver a special message to the person responsible for this act of terrorism. We WILL catch you. Justice WILL be served."* The mayor walked away from the podium through a small gathering of staff members amid camera flashes and reporters calling his name. A voice from an off camera staffer said, *"No questions."*

Fox News had several guests on live. One was a spokesperson for the NRA. He was calm and calculated. Without making direct accusations, he believed the person responsible had a political motive to kill Woolsey. Another guest began shouting, *"It's YOUR fault! You and your damn guns!"*

Tony switched to Bloomberg television. The Heng Seng and the Nikkei were both down sharply in overseas trading. Dow futures were down 700 points, though a connection to the shooting wasn't drawn.

Local news reported a power outage from earlier in the evening. About to switch back to CNN, Tony noticed the image of downed lines. *"We have everything under control,"* a man told the camera. Tony watched as the camera swept across the area illuminated by large portable lights. A tower was on the ground. The image and the comment did not go together. *Cable towers do not fall over.*

He flipped back to CNN, now reporting an angry mob of people outside the mayor's office. More guest panelists offered speculation how various groups would and should respond. Tony turned off the television. Journalism was dead.

Something moved behind him. An immediate sensation of nausea and cold gripped him, realizing someone else was in the room. In a single motion, he dropped to the floor, pulling the pistol from the back of his pants with his right hand, breaking his fall with his left.

Michael stood in the closet wearing the same suit. He slowly held his hands to each side as a gesture.

"What the hell are *you* doing here?" Tony shouted.

BERNIE

The images on CNN gave him purpose, energizing him to do more, fueling his creativity for destruction. The plan had worked. "Don't mess with Bernie Seranov!" he yelled.

LIB

They lay facing each other on the carpet. Bill had kissed her a few times, caressing her arm with his fingers. It was harmless enough, like playing spin the bottle as a kid. His innocence and his tender kisses stirred something inside. It was pleasant and a little titillating. Maybe this was the excitement that an older woman feels with a younger man, though Bill was about her age. No harm in building his confidence a little.

"What're your dreams?" she asked.

"My actual dreams or what I want most in life?"

"Both."

"I sometimes dream of inventions. Once, I dreamed I designed a small power plant that solved the energy crisis."

"How did it work?"

"It used micro-components to operate a small, high efficiency turbine at the point of use."

"Cool. You think it's possible?"

"I do."

"And, what do you want to do?" Lib kept his train of thought moving — fearful that he might drill down into the excruciating details of how the device worked, how it was manufactured, how it might be marketed.

Bill thought for a few minutes. "I would like to live on a gentleman's farm, not far from the city, but far enough."

She couldn't see his face, but she tried to imagine Bill on

a farm. She knew the farm life and it wasn't easy.

"I'd also like to write," he said.

"Excuse me?"

"Yes, I'd like to write." He caressed her arm, brushing the side of her breast while kissing her lightly on her neck. His hand moved to her fingers laying on her stomach, then slid off, barely grazing her abdomen, following the line of her hip and along her thigh.

The tingle of his light touch distracted her for a moment. "Uh . . . what would you write about?"

"I'd start out writing children's books. I have some ideas that might encourage kids to pursue careers in science."

"Really?"

"Yes."

She didn't want to discourage him from writing, but he just didn't seem the type. Suddenly conscious of her breathing, she also didn't want to discourage him from touching her, surprised at her response to his less aggressive approach.

The lights came back on. The enveloping darkness which had allowed them a few moments of intimacy had passed. Face to face, the stark reality of the situation began to set in, lying next to the strange guy she'd seen at the store earlier that day. Somehow, he'd changed into most any other regular person in the darkness. Now, she saw the strange man at the grocery store.

He blinked his eyes.

Momentarily conflicted by her body and mind, she resisted the initial urge to jump up, leaving him alone on the carpet. It didn't seem fair. *Is this the guy that sparked a new desire? Am I the same person in the light that I am in the dark? Is he?* Forcing herself to face her reality began to settle on her. She realized that her discomfort was levied upon her by society. She was no different than all the other hypocrites.

She'd realized her humanity next to this person with hopes and dreams and fears just like the people in the buildings. Why wouldn't she take a few moments out of her busy life? Maybe it was a learning experience. Maybe having an ulterior motive to pick his brain had forced her to look at herself with a critical eye. No, she wasn't ashamed lying next to Bill. She was ashamed that she'd felt ashamed.

"When do I get to see the invisible cloak?" Lib asked, smiling at the paradox.

"I can take you there now, if you want."

"Sure."

TONY

Tony's hands shook as his emotions caught up to his body. He pointed the gun to the side, away from Michael.

"Are you *nuts*?"

"You didn't contact me, so I came to you."

"*Next* time, how 'bout knocking on the *door*. I could've *killed* you."

"We need to talk."

Tony sat up slowly, leaning against the bed with the gun pointed in Michael's general direction.

"If I wanted to hurt you, you wouldn't be here," Michael said as he calmly walked to the love seat and sat.

Tony lifted himself, holding onto the bed. It was either the bed or the love seat. Tony sat on the bed. "Okay, what's going on?"

"A lot. You're right in the middle of it."

"Thanks for the heads up."

"I told you already." Michael probed a hole in the cushion with his finger.

"Well, *next* time, how 'bout sharing a little more information."

"Very well."

Michael pulled several pages of folded paper from inside his jacket. He handed one to Tony.

"This is a composite sketch of the man you're looking for."

Tony looked at the picture. "Why haven't you taken this to the police?"

"Maybe you'll understand soon, I don't know. I can only tell you what I know. The rest is up to you."

"Me?"

"Don't build yourself up, cupcake. If I had my druthers, I'd choose someone a lot smarter and better connected, not to mention better looking."

"Thanks. Has anyone ever told ya that you have an endearing quality?"

Michael handed him a second sheet. "This is a description of another guy who's far more dangerous."

"No sketch?"

"Let's just say he's had some work done."

"So, how do you — they — how do *they* describe someone who's had *work* done?"

"Through actions. It's a profile."

Tony scanned the document. *Speaks at least four languages. Highly educated. Strategic thinker. Extraordinarily elusive. Highly dangerous. Possible ties to Colombia and Mexico.* "This isn't big news. Hundreds of folks fit this description."

"This guy's at the top. His weapon is money."

"Who *are* you really?"

"I've told you, I don't exist."

"Thanks, I feel better now."

"The shooter can lead us to this organization — quite possibly to their leader. They call him Jack."

"This profile is the leader?"

"Yes."

Tony looked at both pages again. The composite sketch looked like thousands of people on the street, a thirty something guy with dark hair and stubble. "He looks

Romanian."

Michael took a pack of cigarettes out of his jacket pocket. "Do you mind?"

"Oh, not at all. Thanks for asking."

Michael lit a cigarette with a silver lighter. "Ashtray?"

Tony walked three steps to the counter of the efficiency apartment and retrieved a plate with crumbs and a small amount of grape jelly.

"Here you are, sir."

Michael blew smoke, seeming content to enjoy the cigarette before speaking.

Tony waited. Michael took several more puffs of the cigarette and then squashed it into the grape jelly on the plate.

"Nice."

"It's a bad habit. What can I say?"

"So, you were gonna tell me something I don't already know."

"Oh, yeah. Almost forgot. These guys don't like us."

"Us?"

"The United States. They want to destroy us."

"Hang on, let me take some *notes*." Tony said, rolling his eyes.

"I'll get to it. They have a belief that democracy will eventually consume itself. They believe that we'll reach a point of critical mass in which we become vulnerable to attack."

"*Wait* a minute. This guy shoots a few people in Chicago and now he's part of a larger scheme to topple the U.S. Government?"

"Well, yeah. Give me a minute, will ya? These guys are strategic. They recognize and understand the weak spots."

"You still haven't answered my question."

"Our government's a mess. Everyday, we read about corruption and the influence of money. We're ripe for the pickin'."

"Our government's *always* been a mess."

"Not at this level. We're in debt to China. Everybody with money has access to our representatives. Meanwhile, people are polarized and angry. We're trying to compete in the global market and we don't have enough jobs. We're a bomb waiting for someone to light the fuse. These are the people who know how to light the fuse."

"Sounds like two guys. I'm still not seeing it."

"There are more than two guys. They're using our own people. I don't know if you're connecting the dots here. So many folks are disenfranchised and angry in our society, it's not hard to find willing participants in this war."

"War? *Really*?"

"Yes, really. It's a cheap way to topple a government. You just need a few guys and the right circumstances for it to work."

Tony sat for a moment, trying to understand the events of the day and the doomsday scenario. He looked at Michael. "I still don't buy it."

"There's a larger plan to destroy the economy. I'm no genius, but I have good reason to believe they're planning to crash the markets at a high level while continuing attacks at the ground level."

"Where are you getting this information?"

Michael didn't answer.

"A few guys are gonna crash the markets," Tony said. "Brilliant."

"I don't understand how it's done, I'm just telling you there's a bigger plan."

Tony shook his head in disbelief. *What if the old man's*

right? Markets have crashed before and recovered. Though 2008 was a close call, he'd not experienced a complete economic collapse like the 1930s. Yes, it could be devastating, but it didn't seem likely. He looked at the old man fiddling with a loose thread on his pants.

"Who're the high level people we're looking for?" Tony asked.

Michael shook his head. "Dunno. But, I suspect they're insiders. The geek can help us find out if we get our hands on the killer."

"So, the killer's just a step toward this other guy and his insiders?"

"Yeah."

The computer geek works for NSA. High level threat to the markets. Maybe the threat's computer-related. Tony thought about recent cyber attacks targeting retail stores and the continuing warnings about cyber security. *Hackers can do a lot of damage, but can they get past all the firewalls and encryption necessary for security*? The thought was unsettling. A breech at that level could have far more impact than any ground level attacks. Yet, the combination of both would have greater potential for destruction, especially if coordinated. Tony glanced at his guest, now staring with his unsmiling face. *Who is this guy*? "What's your last name?" he asked.

Michael tilted his head, looking at Tony from underneath his bushy eyebrows. "LaGuardia."

"Are you with NSA?"

"Nope. Actually, NSA is another sign of trouble. They're overreaching their bounds."

"Homeland Security?"

Michael didn't respond.

"So, what else can you tell me about me?"

Michael appeared deep in thought. Tony waited.

"Your father grew up in this area. Around Wicker Park. A big Cubs fan. He fell on hard times before landing a job down in Cicero. That's where he met your mother. That's where you were raised."

LIB

Bill inserted a key to his upstairs apartment door. Lib heard a dog barking.

"Don't worry, he's harmless."

He opened the door and the dog jumped on his leg. He reached down and picked up the light brown Cocker Spaniel, smiling as the dog licked his chin.

"This is Rex."

"Hi Rex." Lib rubbed the dog's head. Growing up on a farm, Lib could tell a lot about a person from their pets. Most often, animals behave in the same way in which they're treated. She could see that Rex was loved and that Rex loved people. His nub of a tail wagged in response to her, a complete stranger introduced by way of his master. *Complete trust.*

Bill put Rex down and walked into another room. Lib joined the dog on a plain brown sofa rubbing the dog's ears, looking at photos of Bill and his family on a bookcase directly across from her. They looked happy. Bill's mother and father were both good looking people. She read a few of the titles of his books. They varied from classic literature to art to science, perhaps intentionally painting a broader picture of Bill as a person. The books in the living room of her condo were intended as conversation pieces. They, too, were a mix of the interests and areas of expertise that shaped her.

She heard a noise and looked up. She heard it again, this time directly in front of her. Bill's head rose above a line without a body attached, appearing out of nowhere. "Oh my *God*! How *cool*! How *amazing* and *cool*!"

Bill stepped from beyond the substrate material that was his prototype cloak, beaming with pride.

"Are they using your technology now?"

"Yes."

"Then, why is it a secret?"

"They don't want it to leak out and it protects me."

"Makes sense. Did they *pay* you for it?"

"They set up an account that will revert to me in ten years. It's an insurance policy that I won't sell the technology to our enemies."

"Can I ask how *much*?"

"A few million. I'm not sure exactly."

"C'mon. I think you know," she responded before realizing how it might sound. He didn't offer more information. Moments earlier, Bill hadn't seemed capable of making a living, much less designing space age technology.

"I keep it in my office." He reached behind the cloak. Lib heard a click sound, then a silvery screen-like material appeared. "I need to put it back now."

Bill carried the shimmering cloak down the hall of his apartment, the same floor plan as her downstairs unit, except for a longer hall with an extra bedroom which he presumably used as his office. He called to her. Rex jumped down and trotted into the room. Lib followed.

Computer equipment lined two walls along with a cooling unit in the window and a small emergency power supply, all crowding the small room. She sat in a spare office chair as Bill typed a few commands.

Lib's phone buzzed in her purse. Four phone messages

from Tony.

"Bill, you mind if I make a call?"

"No."

Touching *CALL BACK* and listening as Tony's phone rang, she stood and edged around Bill into the doorway, in case she needed to step away for privacy. Bill clicked the CNN icon as Lib watched over his shoulder, waiting for Tony to answer.

"*Hello.*"

"Tony, I haven't listened to your messages. What's up?"

"*You don't know?*"

"No."

Tony described the events to Lib as she leaned against the door, biting her lower lip. Bill's large monitor displayed headlines on CNN.com, confirming Tony's story. He'd submitted his piece to the Trib.

"*Lib?*"

"I'm sorry . . . just thinking."

"*Are you okay?*"

He'd never asked her if she was okay. He sounded genuinely concerned.

"Yeah, I'm fine."

"*Did you learn anything?*"

She thought about the cloak and her promise to Bill. "Not yet."

Bill turned and looked at her. She could see his eyes. He knew something. He knew more than Tony.

"*I met with Michael,*" Tony said.

Lib tried to remember. Tony answered before she could ask. "He's the guy we met at Daley Plaza." The day before yesterday seemed like a long time. He told her about their chat, how he questioned Michael's conspiracy theory.

"Okay. I'll call you back"

"*Get something from the geek.*"

"Okay."

Bill sat, hands together in his lap, repeatedly squeezing a black paper clamp open and allowing it to close, his jaw firmly set. She'd been careful to press the speaker to her ear to prevent Bill from hearing Tony. At least, she thought he couldn't hear.

BILL

He'd read the messages from headquarters and he'd been given new direction. Then, he saw the news. It was happening. All of his training — everything that he'd done came down to this moment. The NSA was very clear in their expectation for him. He had a responsibility.

What would his life be like without complications? He'd reached a critical point in his career at the same time he'd found Lib. He wanted to trust her. He didn't want his work to interfere with his one opportunity in thirty years, though only one day in the making. He wanted her. It was ambitious. He knew the risk of losing, but he had to make an effort. He had to trust that she would not betray him.

"Lib. Please sit down. There's something you need to know."

She put the phone back in her purse and sat directly in front of him in the office chair.

He rehearsed the words he would deliver in his mind. They had to be right.

"I work for the NSA. I'm involved in surveillance that helps our government."

Her eyes opened a little wider.

"Right now, I'm tracking chatter that could be a threat to national security. It will require a lot of my time, but I don't want . . ."

It wasn't coming out right. She put her hand over his

hand which rested on his knee.

" . . . I don't want to walk away for even one minute."

He'd said something that he hoped he wouldn't regret. She looked at him, her head tilted slightly to one side. "It's okay," she said.

He wanted to tell her more. He wanted to tell her how he felt about her. A learned response stopped him. He'd seen the results. He needed to wait. He needed to give her time.

She rubbed his hand, encouraging him to continue.

"Something terrible is happening. I need to respond. But, I want you to know why."

He explained his encryption software. He told her that it was about national security. He told her about the terrorist, though he didn't tell her the man was only a few blocks away.

She gently wrapped her fingers around his hand and squeezed. "I have something to tell you, too. I need you to trust me."

He looked at her. *Oh no. Here it comes.*

"First of all, I like you. I like you a lot."

Bill absorbed the words, an unfamiliar sense of acceptance washing over him.

"I will protect you."

He was confused. "Why?"

Lib shifted in her chair, watching his reaction. "I'm . . . I"m a reporter."

"No! Please tell me that it's not *true*!"

"Bill, please give me a minute."

"You have no *idea*." He stood, then sat back down again. "I cannot *talk* to you!"

"Bill, I won't do anything unless you approve. I promise."

"What do you *mean*? Oh *God*!"

"Please listen to me. I'm not a reporter right now. I'm your friend. I think we can help you."

"*We*?!"

"Yes. Bill, please trust me. This is important. It's more important than any of us."

"*Who*? Who else *knows*?"

"My partner, Tony."

"*Oh God! Oh God!*"

He couldn't believe it! He'd been betrayed. He should have known. It was a classic way to gain information. She was too beautiful. He should have known. He'd lose everything.

"Bill. Take a deep breath. Listen. I *care* about you. I will *not* throw you under the bus. I honestly believe I can *help*."

"I took an *oath*. I'm in violation."

"You're not in trouble if I don't say anything. I'm not going to say anything. But, we need to work with you."

His temples pounded. He wanted to trust her. He'd let her into his apartment. He'd shown her his cloak. She could destroy him.

"There's something else you should know. Someone led us to you."

"*What*?!"

"We got a tip. A guy approached us and told us about you."

How bad can this get? The possibilities overwhelmed him. He just wanted time alone. His meter had expired. There was no more time left on his social energy reserves.

Rex barked in the other room. The doorbell rang.

"Did you order a pizza?" Bill asked.

"No, why?"

"Because they are the only people who ever come to my door."

Bill walked into the living room and peered into the peep hole.

"Who is it?" Lib asked.

"Police. What do they want?"

Bill opened the door.

"William Tee?"

"Yes."

"We need to talk."

LIB

"Excuse me?" Lib said.

The tall policeman spoke to Bill. "Just come with us, we'll straighten everything out at the station."

Rex growled.

"Be quiet, Rex," Bill said.

Lib stood in the living room. She waved at the police officer with a smile, trying to get his attention. "Excuse me, do you have a warrant?"

"Who are *you*?"

Lib hesitated. She didn't want to leverage her position. "My name is Lib Rand. I'm a close friend."

"Lady, *trust* me. It's best if you just stay *out* of it."

The other officer stepped forward with a pair of handcuffs. "I think we need to put these on you just until we get to the station."

"*No*! What did I *do*? Aren't you supposed to *tell* me?"

"Sir, please just cooperate and we'll get it all worked out."

"No. I know my rights. I am *not going*."

"Sir, you're making it hard on yourself."

Rex growled at the officer moving toward Bill with cuffs.

"Lady, please get the dog."

Before Lib could reach him, Rex lunged forward, growling, trying to bite the officer's leg. The officer kicked and sent the dog across the floor. Undeterred, Rex ran back toward the officer who removed a small canister, spraying a stream of liquid, hitting the small dog in the face.

The dog yipped and howled, turning small circles on the carpet.

"*Rex*!" Bill screamed. "You hurt my *dog*!"

"He attacked me."

Lib considered her best course of action. At the moment, that course of action was to stand still and avoid further complication. Rex was probably okay. Bill was *not* okay.

"What did I *do* to you?!" he pled as the officer fastened the cuffs around his wrists.

"Please don't resist them, Bill. I'll get you out."

The policeman led Bill out through the door. She watched through the window as they opened the door to the cruiser parked under a streetlight, pushed his head down, and closed the door.

Lib called Tony. "I need your help."

THE MAYOR

Voices echoed from somewhere off camera.

"*Pat, I'm busy.*"

"*You're always busy, Jacob, I'm trying to help you.*"

The mayors head and torso walked into view. He stopped and turned around. "*Then help me restore order.*"

"*I wanna help you restore order. But, we can't invoke martial law.*"

"*The hell I can't.*" The mayor appeared in full view as he walked around and sat at his desk.

"*Those days are behind us, Jay. People are watching and they'll remember.*"

Mayor Jay Epstein spun a pen on his desk. He looked up and pointed his finger. "*I helped get you elected as Attorney General. I did it as a favor to your father. I expect something in return, Pat.*"

"*That's why I'm here. I'm trying to keep you out of trouble.*"

The mayor cleared his throat but Pat continued, "*I'm getting calls. They're telling me that folks are being picked up and charges aren't being filed. They aren't being mirandized.*"

"*Did you see the news today?*"

"*I did. I can't imagine what that must've been like.*"

"*I'll tell you what it's like. It's like somebody tried to blow my head off and missed.*"

"We have a problem. I agree that we should do more to keep guns out of the hands of lunatics."

The mayor removed his glasses and pinched the bridge of his nose. *"Why do we need guns, Pat?"*

"Jay, we've talked about this. Maybe it seems outdated to you, but it's a guarantee. It's a reminder . . . the people remain a part of our government. Our right to bear arms symbolizes the balance of power between government and ordinary citizens."

"That's bullshit."

"Some folks will disagree with you. I'm not a strong gun advocate, but I respect our Constitution and the guys who understood the forces of government and human nature."

Epstein stood. *"How the hell does a guy like you end up as Attorney General of Illinois?"*

"I guess because of guys like you."

"Your dad, God rest his soul, was a Democrat. What are you?" Epstein said, pointing his finger. *"I'll tell you what you are . . . an independent. What the hell is that?"*

"Actually, on paper you're also an independent."

"That's just some bullshit law you guys passed." Jay turned and looked at the portraits on the wall, away from Pat. *"I had to run as an independent and you know it."*

"We need balance of power. Chicago — and the rest of the country for that matter — needs to back away from political ideologies and do what's right for the people."

Jay turned back to face the AG. *"You think passing a law that makes me run as an independent helps?"*

"In time, yes."

"This city was built on benevolence. It was built on doing the right thing. Difficult decisions must be made. This whole namby pamby business about building consensus is for the birds. Look around."

"*I know, Jay. We have a nice city.*"

Jay slapped the palms of his hands on his desk and leaned forward. "*You damn right it's nice. It's the nicest city on the planet. People love it here.*"

"*Okay, here's something to think about. What happens when the next guy, your successor for example, abuses his power in a way that hurts the city.*"

"*That'll never happen.*"

"*With all due respect, I think it may be happening now.*"

"*I'm gonna pretend you didn't just say that. You can close the door on your way out.*"

BERNIE

"Guns? I don't need no steenkin' *guns*!" Bernie laughed at his version of the Blazing Saddles line.

"What about some C4, Mr. *Mayor*?" Bernie looked at the label on the empty military issue box. "*Wait* a meenute. I can't use C4. Eet's against the *law* for me to have eet." He smiled.

Bernie gently lowered the donut shaped C4 explosive wired to a cell phone onto a rod bolted to a steel base in the bottom of the backpack. The steel base would direct the blast in a hemispherical pattern without the addition of the top plate. Bernie placed a short cardboard tube around the outside of the donut shaped explosive then began to fill the area outside of the cardboard with granulated slag. Slag was dense and had wonderful sharp edges all around, cutting through most anything within a fifty foot radius. Filling the slag to the top of the cardboard, he lifted a steel cone and examined the hole in the center. He lowered the cone — small end down — over the threaded rod until the cone rested on the cardboard tube. He held several large washers, lowering his hand into the cone and placing them over the threaded rod, then used a nut to tighten it down. The steel plate and the steel cone bolted together would direct the blast in the circular pattern he desired.

"Bernie! Deener's ready!"

He gritted his teeth. *Doesn't she understand I'm working down here?*

TONY

Lib's voice had given him a sense of relief.

"I'll pick you up," he'd told her.

Driving to her makeshift apartment, he thought about the article he'd submitted to the editor. He wasn't the most gifted writer, but he felt good about it. He wanted Lib to read the piece, hoping she might appreciate his attention to detail.

Her style was crystal clear, yet expressive and colorful. She could paint images in the reader's mind, seemingly with little effort. She'd laughed at a few of his attempts to write with more style. "It's just not you," she'd told him.

He was plain spoken. *Just the facts, ma'am.* Tony wanted Lib to know that he was capable. There was more to him than declarative sentences. Yet, he'd struggled with the new role of journalism. It had become entertainment rather than delivering information. He was a traditionalist in that way.

This piece felt different. He wanted others to know the impact it had on him. He wanted to share the terror that ran through his body — the realization that someone had just died right before his eyes. The juxtaposition of the Waldorf, nestled on the ultra civilized Gold Coast with a man being murdered required more than simple facts stated in print. It required emotion, something Lib had once explained to him. He'd listened to her. He wanted to show her that he wasn't so far immersed in his manhood to dismiss good advice from a beautiful and knowledgeable woman. He wanted to show his willingness to change. He wanted to experience another side of life — *her* side of life.

Lib waited under a street light at the curb. He pulled up and opened the door for her from inside as the car slowed, allowing just enough inertia to open the door as the car came to a stop.

"Nice trick," she said, sliding into the seat, closing the door behind her.

"I have a few up my sleeve." He smiled at her.

"Bill's at the police station. We need to get him out."

"Why?"

"It was really strange. They wouldn't say."

He glanced at her. He'd asked why to the second comment, not the first.

"He's a good guy, Tony. I don't know what this is about, but I don't think he deserves to be treated this way."

She likes the geek! Tony wanted to turn the car around.

Lib cut her eyes at him, her mouth crooked with suspicion. His face felt hot. *Keep your cool, Tony.* He'd use his contacts to get Bill out, showing compassion and magnanimity, but he would help reveal the truth to her — the truth about the geek and the truth about herself. She wasn't the type to fall for a nerd. *Yeah, she's smart. Yeah, she's Ivy League. But, she likes strength.*

BILL

"I want my phone call!" a man shouted.   At least seventy people stood inside a large holding room at the Milwaukee Street Precinct, no place to sit.   Bill's body trembled — a combined sensory reaction from his surroundings and the events at his apartment. He'd ridden an emotional roller coaster, cresting the highest point with Lib, then speeding downhill. *How could so much happen so fast?   Did Lib check on Rex?   Did she bother to lock his apartment?* He felt violated.

He'd fought the urge to throw up on his ride to the police station — listening to calls on the radio and watching the two officers through the cage with a shotgun and a laptop computer mounted between them. Now, he stood in a room with total strangers, some of whom seemed dangerous, the smell of stale cigarette smoke and sweat nauseating him. One bald guy in a tank top had Chinese tattoos on his neck and shoulders.

The door opened.

"William Tee?"

Thank God. "I'm right here."

"Please step away from the *door* people.   Let 'im through," the uniformed officer advised as Bill edged through the crowd, slipping past sweaty bodies.

"Follow me."

The man led him down a corridor and then into a room with a table. "Please sit down. Can I get you something to eat or drink?"

"No." The man closed the door and locked it.

There were four chairs around a table, but Bill didn't sit in the interrogation room, complete with mirror. *Who could be on the other side*? Though he'd dressed in his nicest Dockers and button down shirt, he felt dirty and looked a little rumpled.

The door clicked and opened. Two men walked into the room. "Please sit down," a man wearing a tie said.

Bill hesitated, then slid a chair back, sitting several feet away from the table.

The man with the tie smiled, placed a file folder on the table and sat down. The other man stood in the corner with his arms folded, wearing a black policeman's uniform and a Kevlar vest.

"I'm sorry for the inconvenience," the man with the tie said. "We're trying to protect people from someone who doesn't belong on the streets."

"Why did you arrest me?"

"We didn't arrest you. You're being detained for questioning."

"I did not do anything."

"The sooner we get through this process, the better." The gentleman with the tie opened the file folder and studied its contents.

"We received several calls about you," he said without looking up. He flipped a page.

"Calls?"

The man looked up. "Several folks reported you."

"*What*?" Bill's face felt hot. He couldn't believe it.

"Apparently, you're a pretty strange guy . . . or, at least that's what your neighbors seem to think."

Bill's mouth opened but no words came out. He wanted

to defend himself, but how? What could he say?

"You mind telling us a little about yourself?"

"I'm Bill Tee. I work at home."

"Who do you work for?"

Bill hesitated. They didn't know. Maybe it would help if he told them.

"I work for the NSA."

The man in the corner shifted his weight and smiled to himself.

"Okay. What do you do for them?"

He was not at liberty to say. It was classified. His position was classified. *Oh God*!

The man with the tie looked back down at the folder. "It says here that you're on Zoloft."

Bill felt the blood flowing to his face. *That information is protected*!

"Wasn't the shooter in Connecticut on Zoloft?" the man in the tie called over his shoulder, the officer nodding in response.

What is happening?! "I want to talk to a lawyer."

The door opened. A woman in uniform motioned to the man in the tie. He stood and she whispered something.

The door closed. The man with the tie smiled briefly, changing quickly to a stern look. He slammed his palm on the table. "Where were you today at noon!!?"

They think I am the shooter! How did this happen? "I was . . . ," he struggled to catch his breathe. An anxiety attack. He tried to speak but his pulse raced wildly. *Just calm down. It's just anxiety. Let it pass*.

"What's *wrong* with you, *boy*?" the man in the tie screamed in his face. "You look *crazy*!"

TOM AND GEORGE

"You know, Georgie, a wise man once said, 'Rightful liberty is unobstructed action according to our will within limits drawn around us by the equal rights of others.'"

"That's a whole lotta words."

"It means our freedom should not extend beyond the rights of those around us."

"Some folks are really full of themselves. *Here's* one for ya. 'It is better to be alone than in bad company.'"

"Funny."

"Yeah, I thought you might like that one."

BILL

Bill couldn't breathe. He wanted to go home. He remembered Lib, regaining his composure. He was with Lib. The door opened again. This time a man in a suit whispered to the man in the tie and then walked away. The man in the tie and the man in the uniform both walked out behind him, leaving the door open.

Can I leave? Something didn't make sense to him. *Are people watching? What am I supposed to do?*

Bill stood, placing his hand on the table to brace himself.

The man with the suit came back and stood in the doorway. "C'mon. Your friends are here."

Lib stood at the end of the hallway next to a large man, her hand over her mouth. She ran down the hall, throwing her arms around him. Bill stood with his head lowered, arms by his side.

"I know you've been through a lot and I know you've every right to be angry, but please trust me," Lib whispered.

"Is Rex okay?"

"Rex is fine."

He fought the emotion. He told her about the holding room with all the greasy, smelly people. He told her about the man with the tie. "I don't know why this happened to me."

She wiped a tear from her cheek. "You're a very special, wonderful person. You haven't done anything wrong . . . "

Her voice cracked. " . . . but I want you to know that you're not alone in this world." Her lips trembled as she held his drooping shoulders with her hands, tilting her head up to look into his eyes. "Don't let these bastards get you *down*, do you *hear* me?!" He nodded.

She wrapped her arms around him and held him close, her head against his chest.

The man cleared his throat, one hand stretched toward them, his other hand extended toward the door. "C'mon guys, let's get outta here," Lib's reporter friend said.

LIB

Tony was quiet driving back to her place. He flashed a knowing look at her in the rearview mirror several times. Bill sat in the front seat, his arm resting on the door, staring out of the passenger window.

The car stopped at the curb.

"I'll call you later," Lib said to Tony as Bill helped her from the back seat.

The Camaro rumbled back onto the street and disappeared around the corner.

"Let's go in," she said.

Retrieving the keys from her purse, Lib unlocked the door, letting Bill enter the apartment ahead of her. He stood in the living room area, staring at darkness through the sliding glass doors.

She locked the door, noticing her reflection in the glass, approaching him from behind, reaching for his hand.

"No, in here." She gently led him down the short corridor, lit only through the partially closed door to the bathroom. He stood with his arms down by his side. She turned him toward her and looked up at his face, barely visible in the shadows. Holding his face with one hand, she kissed him softly on the mouth and then on both cheeks and on his stubbly chin. This would not be the frantic, impassioned moment she'd experienced with other lovers.

She put her free hand on his chest, nimbly working the

top button through the buttonhole of his shirt. She moved slowly to the next button, deliberately taking her time as she alternated kissing his lips and his face. Opening the top of his shirt, she used both hands to caress his chest, moving her face down, kissing his neck. She felt him breathing.

He touched her hair with both hands. She stood to meet his mouth, this time exploring, softly, gently. She leaned away from him and lifted her sweater over her head. In a few motions, she lowered the straps of her bra, lifting and turning to unhook it, dropping it to the floor, feeling the weight of her breasts and exposure to the air. She pressed against his chest, feeling his skin and his warmth.

Lib unbuttoned his pants as she kissed him full on the mouth, sliding pants and underwear down around his hips, her hands caressing.

"Sit down," she whispered.

He sat on the inflated air mattress. She untied his shoes and pulled his pants, underwear and shoes off in a bundle. "Lay back and relax."

Lib stood, kicked off her shoes, removed her pants and panties, then lay close beside him, feeling his naked body against hers.

* * *

Wan light filtered through gently moving trees outside the window, slowly revealing the bare room to a new day. They lay on twisted sheets, sweating, breathing together. Lib was no longer ashamed. It felt good to lie naked in his arms without remorse. He had responded to her — never saying a word — his slow hands caressing and tingling her skin, never making a sound except for his breathing.

"Are you okay?" she mumbled into his chest.

"Yes. I am good."

"Yes. You *are*."

She teased his nipple with her tongue.

"I hope you trust me now," she said.

He didn't say anything.

"Please, just talk to me for a little while."

He breathed deeply. "Okay."

She waited. He would talk when he felt ready.

They listened to the sounds of the city waking up. A car horn blared in traffic. A bus engine roared. A helicopter hovered in the distance. They lay together without regard of time, listening, breathing. Relieved of the pressure to fill the air with her words, she could wait for him as long as it took, hearing the thump of his heart.

"I don't want another day like yesterday," he said. "I just want people to like me."

"I like you."

"I don't know why it's so hard. I don't know why I struggle to say the right thing."

She made little circles with her finger, playing with tufts of hair on his abdomen.

"It's okay. I like what you say."

"They had my medical records. There is something you should know about me."

"Um hm." She caressed his chest.

"I see a psychiatrist a few times a year."

"So?"

"I have anxiety attacks."

"A lot of people have anxiety attacks. It's no big deal."

"I'm different than most people."

Lib lifted and smiled at him. "That's not always a bad thing."

"I have Asperger's."

"I know," she said.

TONY

Tony rolled onto his back, dust particles sparkling in the sunlight that beamed through his window. He'd dreamed about Lib, smiling and laughing.

It made him sick to think about her and the geek. He'd helped Bill, phoning his contacts at police headquarters, so what does she do? He didn't know what happened after he'd dropped them off, but he saw the way she embraced him at the police station.

"Good morning."

"*Jeez*!" Tony jumped at the sound next to his bed, Michael, sitting on the love seat. "You coulda' given me a *heart* attack! Don't you believe in *knockin'*?"

"I read your piece in this morning's *Trib*. Nice work."

"So, now you're an *editor*."

"Among other things."

Tony slid out of bed, holding a bed sheet around his body. "You mind if I get *dressed*?"

"Go ahead."

"Maybe you could turn your *head* or something?" Tony waited for a moment and then shook his head, dropping the sheet on the floor. "You want a show, I'll give it to ya big guy."

"Not much to see, cupcake."

Tony selected a clean pair of khakis and a button down, then put them on. He had a closet full of 'em.

"Where's your girlfriend?"

"She ain't my girlfriend. She's a coworker."

"Yeah, right."

"What *is* it with you? This is *my* place, now I'm answering *your* questions?"

"I think she likes you, but you're not exactly a prize."

"Well, you ain't so great yourself, *mister*."

Michael pulled out his cigarettes. "You mind?"

"Are you *kidding*?! Go *ahead*!"

He lit a cigarette and blew a few smoke rings. "It's a nasty habit."

"You said that already."

"Mind if I turn on the TV?"

Tony shook his head in disbelief. "Knock yourself out."

Michael picked up the remote and turned on a television that rested on a makeshift table of concrete blocks and unfinished shelving board in the corner. Tony winced at the sound of oohs and ahhs, accompanied by skin slapping together and the image of a man screwing a woman on the hood of a car.

"You know you can go blind."

"Dude!!" *How invasive can this guy be?*

Michael flipped through a few channels, a great relief to Tony who wasn't in the mood for watching porn in his apartment with a stalker at 9 a.m.

CNN continued to follow developments in Chicago. A large crowd had gathered at Daley Plaza. People held signs, some supporting the ban on guns, others against. People shouted at each other as police officers on horses kept them separated.

"*Emotions are running high at Daley Plaza*," the lady reporter shouted above the noise with the crowd behind her. She used one hand holding a microphone to brush aside brown strands of hair that had blown in front of her face while holding a small monitor to her ear with the other hand. *"Police are calling for the crowd to disperse, threatening to arrest people."*

BOOOMMMM!!! The camera shook, quickly panning across buildings, then transmitting images of shadows on passing concrete as the cameraman ran with the live camera pointed at the ground, voices screaming. *"Stop, you need to get this!"* the reporter said off camera. The camera lifted back up, now further away, shakily zooming in. People lay on the ground in pools of blood. A policeman squirmed, his leg pinned beneath a dead horse.

"Oh my *God*!" Tony shouted. Michael sat stone faced, cigarette held between his fingers.

Wolf Blitzer tried to get the attention of the reporter then spoke directly to the camera. *"We've witnessed a horrific event at Daley Plaza in Chicago. It's obvious that many people are hurt and possibly dead, but we want to remain respectful of families. The images you saw were broadcast live, so we offer our apologies along with our thoughts and prayers to those impacted by this act of terror."*

Michael sat without emotion. He stubbed the cigarette into the same dish on the arm of the love seat where he'd left it the night before.

"I believe we may have someone inside at Daley Center," Wolf continued.

The mayor stood at a podium with a group of men around him. *"Ladies and gentlemen,"* he began, *"just minutes ago, a bomb detonated outside of this building at Daley Plaza. Please, we urge everyone to exercise caution. If you're in the area, we urge you to remain indoors until we secure the scene."* His lips drawn into a thin straight line, he paused, regaining his composure. *"We have a sketch."* The mayor held the same sketch that Michael had given Tony of the dark haired man, the camera zooming in. *"If anyone has seen this man, please contact us at the number shown on the screen. Do not approach him, he's considered armed and dangerous."*

Michael glanced at Tony out of the corner of his eyes. The lady reporter interviewed witnesses.

"It's getting bad, cupcake."

Tony couldn't shake the images of people dying on an otherwise beautiful sunny morning in Chicago. It just didn't seem possible. The truth was stranger than fiction.

BILL

CNN.com reported forty eight people dead, dozens more injured in the blast.

He entered the URL for the private site used by his agency for communications. After entering his user name and password, a text message popped up.

"*Where have you been?*"

BIll tapped a response.

"*Sorry, I was detained by police.*"

"*We'll talk about that later. We need you to focus on your JOB!*"

"*Yes sir.*"

"*This is our last chance to find Jack before they get to the Romanian. He's all we've got.*"

Bill could see Lib's reflection in the monitor, peering over his shoulder. Her eyes widened.

"You know where he *lives*?" she whispered.

"Yes."

"We've got to *stop* him," she whispered again.

"It is okay, they cannot hear us."

"Oh."

"It is complicated. My job is to gather and deliver information."

"*Augh*! I cannot be*lieve* our government sits and *allows* this guy to murder innocent *people*!"

"They want his boss."

"Who's his boss?"

Bill turned in his seat, facing her.

"Nobody seems to know, but we call him Jack. He is a very dangerous man."

"Tell me where the shooter lives."

"No."

She put her hand on his arm. "Bill. We've got to *do* something. He'll kill again."

"I know."

"Doesn't it *bother* you?"

"Yes."

"Then let's *do* something about it."

"I'll lose my job."

"*God*! That's in*fur*iating!"

Lib stood up with her hands on her hips. "We could use the *cloak*."

"*No*!"

"Bill, we can use it to install a surveillance camera." Lib paused. "*Wait* a minute. You already *have* surveillance, *don't* you?"

He hesitated. Previous attempts at lying had proven disastrous — always getting caught, ending up on the bottom of the pile. The truth was simple. Nothing to remember.

"Yes."

"Please, let me see."

Bill turned toward the computer, pulling up one of several recorded surveillance images on his computer. It showed a still image of a house like so many other houses in Chicago — a craftsman styled bungalow built in the '40s — similar to his home as a boy growing up in Oak Park.

Bill started the video and they watched as a Honda CRV turned into the driveway of the house, pulling up to a detached garage in the back yard. A man with dark hair got out of the car, carrying what looked like a shopping bag into the house, disappearing out of view, no doubt entering the house from the back as a vintage Camaro drove slowly down the street.

"That's *Tony's* car!" Lib said.

"This is not good."

"How old is this video?"

Bill looked at the time stamp. "About two hours."

The image stopped.

"What happened?"

"The software stops until something moves."

He clicked another thumbnail, minutes later.

Tony appeared on the left side of the screen, walking on the sidewalk in front of the house. He passed casually — until disappearing out of the camera's range on the right side of the screen. The image stopped again. Bill clicked the next file, selecting play on the screen. It was ninety seconds later.

Tony crept into view on the right side, standing in the bushes between houses.

"Don't *do* it, Tony!" Lib said.

He stepped through the hedge and peered into a first floor window. The dark haired man appeared on the opposite side of the house — carrying a long, slender object.

"Oh my *God*!"

Tony stood near the house. They watched in horror as the dark haired man crept along the front of the house, peering around the corner at Tony, leaning over to look through a basement window.

"I can't *look*!"

The man approached Tony from behind, swinging the long object. Tony fell to the ground. The man dragged Tony toward the back of the house and around the corner. The video stopped.

"We've got to *do* something!" Lib said, her hand over her mouth.

"I cannot.   But, you can give the information to the police as long as you don't tell them where you got it."

"They'll ask questions.   They won't respond quickly enough."

"Lib, Tony is probably dead."

"I can't sit and do *nothing*! I have to do *some*thing!"

Lib picked up her purse and started toward the door.

"*Wait*! I will go with you.

BERNIE

"Tony Wochowski. What a pleasant surprise."

Tony sat in the dim light from the monitors across the room — arms and hands stretched behind him, bound together with wire ties — duct tape around his ankles and around his drooping head, covering his mouth.

"Perhaps we can chat later. I am very beezy right now."

Bernie returned to his monitors displaying an office, a school building, Daley Plaza and several images around the house where he'd seen Tony step through the hedges. Tony would soon die, perhaps after a short lecture. *Isn't that what they do in American movies?*

Tony groaned.

"Not now, Tony. I'm trying to decide who to *keel* today . . . besides *you*, of course."

"Let's check the *noose*. We have the *left* wing CNN. Then, we have the *right* wing Fox Noose. I just want to know what ees going on around the *warld*. I don't *want* opinion. *Right* Tony?"

Tony groaned and squirmed.

"Ah, *here's* sometheeng."

" . . . *an incendiary device was discovered in Washington last night as protesters gathered in front of the Capitol*."

"I *love* theese country! So pre*deek*table!"

He stood with a revolver in his right hand. Tony looked at him wearily. Bernie, the matador, regarded his opponent, head turned ninety degrees from his sideways stance, pistol at his side. He moved his body one hundred eighty degrees, his head facing Tony through the turn. Facing his prisoner, he marched forward one step at a time then stopped, erect with rigid discipline, chest out and chin back, one arm's length from his target. Raising the pistol flatways, he aimed at trembling, wincing eyes, looking away, preparing.

Bernie relaxed his body and lowered the pistol, leaning his face down.

"Wake *up*! Wake *up*! The *warld* ees on fire! Ha, ha, ha, ha! What's zee *matter* Tony? Theese ees *fun*, no?

Bernie tilted his head to look at Tony's wide eyes.

"So *tee*pical. I talk to people, they don't talk back to me. Maybe it's my strange accenation. No, maybe eets because Americans are so *full* of theemselves!!!

"Mmmphh, um nnt."

"Excuse me? Can't you see that I am *talking* here? You people have so much but you complain and you fight. You fight and you complain. Have you ever been *hungry*? Do you realise what a preevileged *class* you are een?"

Tony's eyes showed pain. Remorse perhaps.

"Everybody leeves the great American dream. Wark hard and you weel get ahead, no?"

Bernie paused for effect, standing at an angle.

"Een my country, I have equeevalent of two PhD's. Here, I wark in security, designing and eenstalling seestums. Do I look like a good ol' *boy*? I become seeteezen. Then, you open your barders and *geev it all away*!!!"

"Mmmmphhhhh!"

"Ah. So maybe you, too. I am soo happy to see how it comes apart in your hands. You greedy bastards desarve eet."

Tony moved in his chair. Again, Bernie pointed the

pistol at Tony's head. "*BANG*!" Bernie shouted. Tony flinched. "Ha, ha, ha, ha! You are afraid to *die*, no?"

A buzzer sounded. Bernie looked over his shoulder then quickly returned to his chair in front of the monitors. A tall, slender man walked on the sidewalk in front of the house.

Tony squirmed and moaned.

"I'll be right back, Tony." Bernie ran the stairs two at a time with the pistol held head high. *Tony may soon have company.*

Opening the back door and stepping outside, he looked in both directions, then moved to the corner of the house — peeking around toward the front. The man was not visible from where he stood. He edged along the side of the house, now holding the pistol with two hands. *Where is he? Maybe just someone out for a walk.*

LIB

The dark haired man walked right past her — his pistol passing within a few feet of her face. She trusted the cloak, but her heart pounded in her chest as she moved slowly toward the back. The killer had stopped at the corner of the house as she walked carefully in her sock feet. One noise could bring him back, losing her only opportunity. She opened the back door, stepping inside and closing it quietly behind her.

Bill had known that Bernie, the Romanian man, worked in security, correctly assuming that the house would be monitored and alarmed. Lib had to find Tony, use the cloak to cover them both, and then wait for Bill's second diversion.

The door to the basement was open. *Maybe Tony's downstairs. God, let him be alive*! A step creaked under her foot, something to remember, third from the top. Continuing down, she could see the monitors. Another step creaked. Number two from the bottom. She saw the shop area, lit only by the monitors, Tony sitting on a chair partially obscured by her shadow.

"Tony," she whispered.

"Mmmphhhh?"

"It's *me, Lib*."

"Umm mmphhhh?"

"Please don't be alarmed, I'm wearing a cloaking device. I'm right in front of you." She lowered the cloak to reveal her face, then unwrapped it. Tony's eyes widened. Lib rolled the cloak and stood it in the corner next to a shop stool.

"He'll be right back, so we need to act fast. We'll find a place to stand with the cloak around us until we have a chance to escape. Got it?"

"Rurr mmnnn nnnn!" Tony nodded his head frantically. Lib held her finger to her lips then pulled the duct tape quickly from his mouth.

"He's got a *gun*," Tony whispered.

Lib jerked her finger back to her lips and glared at Tony. She retrieved a utility knife from a nearby workbench, cutting the wire ties then searching the room frantically for a place to hide as Tony removed the tape binding his ankles to the chair. An old white chest freezer sat against the opposite wall. Opening it, Lib stared in horror at a woman's frosty body curled in a fetus position, illuminated by a light in the freezer door. She lowered the door gently, her hands shaking.

The back door opened above them followed by brisk footsteps to the top of the basement stairs. The top step creaked . . . then the other. They stood huddled together in the open space between the lathe and the drill press, the cloak wrapped around them. She'd looked under the shop table, but opted for the open space. She could feel Tony controlling his breathing . . . slowly out, slowly in. She did the same.

She watched as Bernie sat at the computer desk, no doubt looking for Bill on the monitors. If only Bernie would go back upstairs, she'd text Bill to let him know where they were in the house and that Tony was alive.

Bernie turned then jumped up from his chair. He ran the steps and across the floor to the back door before his footsteps abruptly turned and came back across, stopping at the top of the steps.

"Tony? Are you okay down there in the *dark*!" The fluorescent lights flickered on. Lib's heart pounded in her chest.

The upper stair tread squeaked. A few seconds later the lower stair tread squeaked.

Bernie ran to the center of the shop area — looking around frantically. "Okay, so you want to die *now*?" He looked under the bench. Behind the hot water heater. Behind the chest freezer. Directly at them. Up in the floor joists. He waved his pistol around. "Come out, come out, wher*ever* you are."

Bernie walked back to the other side of the basement near the monitors. He looked under the stairs and around the work table.

"I know you're een here *some*where."

Bernie made another pass around the shop, waving his pistol. He looked down at the floor where pieces of duct tape laid around the chair.

"Maybe you have a knife. Maybe you freed yourself wheen I went outside. If I were you, what would I do? I'd crawl through the basement window."

Bernie inspected the window. "The cobwebs and leaves are undisturbed. Maybe you weent upstairs."

Bernie walked to the stairs but hesitated. Instead, he walked to the monitors and sat, double clicking the mouse on an icon. On the screen, he watched himself walking around the house. He double clicked another file. He watched himself walk into the house from the basement. *He had a camera mounted in the house! Maybe he had cameras mounted in the basement! He'll see us together*!

Lib felt Tony move. She poked him. Stepping through

the back side of the cloak, Tony walked into the center of the room, arms raised.

"*Here* I am."

Bernie walked to him, pistol raised.

"You are too much trouble! Seet *down*!"

Tony sat in the chair. Bernie pointed the pistol at Tony's temple. "Where were you hiding?"

Tony didn't respond.

"Who ees outside?"

Tony still didn't respond.

Bernie pulled the hammer back with his thumb until it clicked.

"I will give you three seconds."

"One."

"Two."

He won't do it, Lib thought. *He's worried about the other person,*

"Three."

Bernie walked around in a wide circle, watching Tony sweat profusely. *No, Tony! Stay cool.*

"What ees the *matter* Tony?   What ees *both*ering you, eh?"

Bernie continued to watch Tony as he changed his direction. "Are we a*lone*?" He pointed the gun at Tony's head.

Tony jiggled his knee for a split second.

POW! Lib winced at the echo and recoil of the 9 mm held in her shaking hand. Bernie dropped to the floor, facing her, his eyes searching, searching. She dropped the cloak and stepped closer to him, his gaze now locked on her. Blood began to spread on the floor beneath his chest, crimson rivulets streamed from his nose and the corner of his open mouth — his eyes fixed and dull.

She kicked his arm. No movement. She kicked it again and his pistol slid away. No movement. Tony stepped over Bernie's outstretched arm and retrieved the pistol.

BILL

There was something about the man leaning against the badly rusted 1974 Ford LTD, two doors down from Bernie's. They'd met once before. He'd just showed up at his apartment and invited himself in. He'd made Bill uncomfortable with his easy manner that day and now once again demonstrating an odd coolness following the noise from Bernie's house.

"How're your friends doing?" he asked as Bill approached him.

"I think they are in trouble." It was not his best option, but Bill needed help and he needed it fast. Maybe the man knew how to solve his problem.

"Let's go check it out."

"No, wait. You don't understand. Surveillance cameras and alarms are all over this place."

Ignoring Bill, Michael walked casually toward the house, looking straight ahead, walking and talking as Bill ran to catch up. "I once rescued three Cuban hostages from a booby trapped house down in Havana. I cut a few wires to enter the house and slit a guy's throat with a straight razor. Blood squirted into a bowl of rice, onto the table, onto an old refrigerator and on the stove as the guy spun around holding his throat. It was a mess. Ruined my Ron Jon shirt."

Michael used his elbow to break a window pane on the back door, opened it and then crunched through the glass, down the hallway to the open basement door. Bill followed — looking around.

"We're down *here*." Lib called. Bill followed slowly behind Michael who walked down the stairs.

By the time Bill could see into the shop, the old man had already stooped over Bernie's body. "Nice work."

Lib ran into Bill's arms as Tony watched with a blank look on his face.

Bill smoothed Lib's hair. "Is he dead?" he asked.

"Yep," the man said, now rummaging through a drawer — retrieving a pair of tin snips.

"We'll probably need his thumbprint for encryption," he said, lifting Bernie's lifeless hand and snipping off the end digit of his thumb, residual blood staining the shears.

Bill pointed to the monitors. "His computer's right here."

"So it is." He handed the thumb to Bill. "You may need this. I think it's your key."

Bill pinched Bernie's thumb in his fingers and then put it in his pocket.

"Hey guys, look over here," Lib said.

She'd opened the chest freezer.

Bill, Tony and Lib stared inside. "The truth is stranger than fiction," Tony said.

TONY

Bill opened the door for Lib and then walked around to the driver's side of his Prius. He waved at them. Tony didn't wave back.

They'd loaded the computer equipment into Bill's car. Decoding was long, hard work and it would be much easier back at his apartment, Bill had said. A few items from the detached garage were divided between the LTD and the Camaro.

Computer geeks. To hell with 'em, Tony thought as he watched Bill and Lib drive away.

"Didn't quite work out the way you wanted eh, cupcake?"

"Plenty more where she came from."

They leaned against Tony's Camaro. "You mind if I smoke?"

"Yeah, Michael, I mind," Tony said in a deadpan voice. "Please don't light that cigarette around me."

Michael lit the cigarette with his silver lighter.

"I think they make a nice couple."

"Go to hell."

Michael exhaled a plume of smoke.

"I'm not one to give advice . . ."

"Then *don't.*"

" . . . but, sometimes it's good to sacrifice something you care about."

"What're you talking about?"

Michael exhaled another plume of smoke.

"What do you love, Tony?"

Tony didn't respond.

"Yourself?"

Tony smirked and turned his head away.

"It's okay. Everybody loves themselves. But, who or what else do you love? Money?"

"I don't know. I've never had any."

"What about Lib?"

"What *about* her?"

"Do ya love 'er?"

"Yeah. Okay. I *said* it. Why don't you leave me alone?"

"What else?"

Tony glared at Michael as he stomped out the half smoked cigarette. "Sorry, it's a bad habit."

"I love my country. I love Chicago and the Cubs. That's about it."

"Hmmmm."

A small boy on a bicycle pedaled past them.

"Well, what?" Tony asked.

"Ever wonder what goes through a guy's mind when he's about to die fighting for his country?"

Tony kicked at the grass.

Michael continued. "I have good reason to believe they've resolved themselves at that point. Sure, some are terrified. But, many are willing to make the sacrifice. They know it's over. They're looking forward to their just reward."

"Right."

"It's not so bad on the other side, cupcake."

"What do you know about the other side?"

"More than I can explain with words."

"What's *up* with you, man? And, what's up with all this talk of *sacrifice* and the other *side*?"

"I'm just trying to prepare you, son."

"For *what*?"

Michael stood, eternally stone faced. "For the inevitable."

"What's *that* supposed to mean?"

"Death."

"I've seen enough death these past two days."

"*Your* death, Tony."

It was the first time Michael had called him by name.

"You really know how to cheer a guy up, don't you?"

"The point is, the very moment that you let go of your fear, you can live free."

"That's easier said than done."

"The soldier sacrificing his life discovers the freedom of letting go for a few seconds, or maybe even a minute or two. Think of what could happen if you let go of that fear right now. You'd be surprised at what you can accomplish with that level of freedom."

"Right."

Michael looked back at Bernie's house, two doors down. "You think that's enough?"

"Yeah."

Michael dialed his cell. They heard breaking glass as large flames shot out of all the windows. They'd disconnected two gas lines, allowing natural gas to fill the space. "I'll see ya later."

"Okay."

* * *

He'd passed a fire truck several miles away from

Bernie's pyre. It would take the forensics team months to work through the rubble. Better that way. Michael had retrieved the 9 mm slug out of a floor joist, following blood splatter where Lib had fired the weapon through Bernie's chest. He'd found spalled concrete on the wall where the bullet ricocheted, judging the upwards angle to a shallow hole in the wood. He'd also wiped the doorknobs. Besides, a police investigation wouldn't help anyone at this point. Well, maybe it would give some closure to a few grieving families. They could grow from the experience.

The Sears Tower gleamed in the early summer sunlight. The men who designed the tower were gone, but their legacy remained part of the iconic Chicago skyline.

What have I accomplished?, Tony thought as he passed the Chicago Theater on State. He tried to dismiss the old man and his crazy talk, but something gnawed deep down in the pit of his stomach, something that even a cheeseburger and fries couldn't remedy. He wanted something that he couldn't understand. Was it a feeling of belonging? His friends had all married. They were too busy with family to hang out. The kids at the Boy's Club on Saturdays changed each week. They didn't stick around. *So much for giving back to the community.*

Maybe he'd move south. He'd heard stories and had visited Florida a few times. His image of the South was based on movies and television shows, few of which were flattering.

He considered becoming a full blown alcoholic — like Nick Cage in Leaving Las Vegas. Elisabeth Shue might be a nice addition. Nah. Too dark.

What if Michael was right? *What if we're liberated by our resignation to death?* Sounds good on paper, but it wasn't an easy pill to swallow. *Who could do it?*

Tony wasn't a hero. He was more of an opportunist. He wanted the easy, low hanging fruit. Folks with principles and opinions struggled through life, trying to match their actions with their belief systems. For Tony, it was easier to live without a belief system. He would bend like the willow. He would roll with the punches and do as the Romans do, believing whatever he wanted to believe. So why wasn't he getting anywhere? How's it possible for a mostly unprincipled man to feel anything, let alone the weight of his own existence? Something didn't make sense. Somehow, the whole notion of living large and free seemed empty and depressing.

BILL

Unloading and unpacking after a long night, Bill and Lib sat on office chairs amid empty boxes and computer equipment.

"We can do this together," Lib said. Her hair was tousled. She'd said very little about the events leading them to their task of setting up equipment. Bill worried about her. She seemed distant and her smile had faded.

Bill reached down and rubbed Rex's ear. The poor dog attached himself to Bill's foot on the floor. "What if we find sensitive information?" Bill wondered how to justify stealing the computers from a dead man's house. "How will we explain the fire?"

"We don't have to reveal our sources."

"I may have signed a non-disclosure."

"Yeah, but *I* didn't. Stop worrying."

Going AWOL in a moment of crisis would not look good. Bill had to find a new job. He'd saved some money, but he didn't like dipping into savings to pay living expenses.

"Where will I go? I do not mix well into the general population."

"I'll ask around. We'll find something for you, probably better than working for NSA."

Sliding from her chair onto one of the few available spots on the carpet, Lib lay next to Rex as the dog licked and chewed something beneath Bill's chair.

Bill felt a slight tinge of panic as he surveyed the obstructed path to the door. He didn't like tight spaces, particularly when surrounded by people. He watched Lib petting Rex for a moment with her eyes closed. When he looked again, she was asleep.

Though tired and emotionally drained, he felt energized by solitude. It was his most productive time — and he'd learned to make good use of it. The information stored inside the black computer cabinets arranged on the floor intrigued him. *What is in there? What will I find out about this horrible man?* He imagined Bernie's charred body beneath the smoldering rubble.

In truth, the prospect of finding information about Bernie and Jack remained important to him. It was part of his training, but apart from his recent career blunder, he felt a responsibility as an ordinary citizen. He also felt strongly drawn to Bernie's thought process. The blimp and other strange contraptions found in the detached garage were of great interest to Bill. He wanted to pick Bernie's brain post mortem through stored data on his computers laying in pieces around him.

He needed a plan of attack. Using his computer as the hub through which to retrieve data via USB was risky. His computer was secure and it contained sensitive information. It made more sense to use one of Bernie's CPUs as the hub. Actually, it made sense to find out which CPU Bernie had already used as the hub.

He needed more space. Bill stood and selected a path for his feet as he lifted and removed empty boxes to the dining area, taking great care to step over Lib. He was quiet and deliberate, moving slowly around the dog, Lib, and the equipment on the floor.

Lib murmured, her eyebrows knit together, eyes dancing

behind closed eyelids. *So beautiful, even in her sleep.* She moaned. "No!" She spoke to a threat — some demon in her mind. He wanted to wake her, to soothe her with comforting words, but she needed this process of elimination, purging the emotions collected throughout her difficult day. It was a healing time for her — a time he would not disturb.

Boxes of cables intimidated most folks, but it looked to Bill like toy blocks. He barely thought of his task as he inserted the end of several cables quickly behind one of the CPUs. It would take a few minutes to get in and make sense of it, but Bill's mind was on the surveillance systems and the inventions. It was his Christmas morning.

Within minutes, Bernie's system was connected. Bill flipped on the power and watched. A special screen appeared requiring some form of passcode. Perhaps it wanted Bernie's thumb image on the small peripheral device plugged into one of the USBs. Bill reached into his pocket and fumbled around. He checked his other pocket. Bernie's thumb was gone! Maybe it fell out. He looked around. The dog still chewed something on the floor. "*Rex!*" The dog whimpered and looked up, Bernie's thumb lying between his front paws. "*Bad dog!*" Lib murmured and rolled over as Bill retrieved the mangled thumb and inspected it. The cut end was in shreds and a bone was now partially protruding. A few punctures were on the pad. He wouldn't know if it would deliver enough positive points to gain access until he tried it.

Taking a deep breath, Bill pressed the severed thumb against the device. The screen displayed a message. "*WELCOME TO HELL*".

THE MAYOR

Mayor Epstein looked at his watch. He wasn't comfortable asking favors from Pat, but he needed help. Things weren't going well.

"*Jay*!" Pat's voice echoed through the cavernous main hall of the Field Museum.

"Keep your voice down, will ya?" Epstein wore a Cubs hat and sunglasses. He looked like a tourist.

"What's up?" Pat had an unusual knack of blowing past confrontation as though it never existed — no doubt a necessity for the Attorney General of Illinois.

"Let's go to the coffee shop."

They walked past the enormous African elephant into the museum cafe and stood in line among patrons.

"You look nice," Pat offered.

Being mayor had plenty of great perks. Anonymity was not one of them. But, Jay Epstein considered himself accessible to the people — frequently showing up in public locations around the city. It was actually a relief. He liked going outside — enjoying all of the great spots of Chicago. Perhaps in part, he wanted the recognition to show that he wasn't afraid, though the museum was one of those places where folks didn't bother him much. The Chief of Police had suggested closing the museums and Jay had refused. Besides, the patrons were mostly tourists, many having no idea that he was mayor of the Second City. Setting an example was hardly worth the effort at the museum. Perhaps a Cubs game with a few cameras to capture the moment would be better.

They both ordered regular coffee and waited.

"I need a favor," Epstein said.

"Uh oh. Here it comes."

They retrieved their coffees from the end of the counter and walked to a table at the far end with a clear view of fifty or so people gathered in the main hall, including some Catholic kids in uniform.

"I gotta get a handle on things," Epstein said, sipping his coffee.

"It's not an easy job you have."

"It's not so bad for the most part. I'm treated well. I get plenty of respite between confrontations."

"What can I do?"

"You can help me — at least for the short term. I'll take the heat later, but I need to prolong our current strategy."

Pat sipped his coffee, seeming to consider the mayor's proposal. "You know, Jay, we're all headed for something." He played with a plastic stir stick. "We're gonna see more of the same thing we've seen this week. It's the same in the other big cities."

Jay rolled his eyes. He braced himself for the spiel, but it was necessary to hear Pat out. It was part of the process. Give them time to vent their frustration and look for the common ground after the steam dies down a bit.

"Our justice system is failing."

"I don't like to hear that from the AG."

"Well, strictly off the record, I believe it's true." Pat sipped his coffee again before continuing. "I wanna go after the gangs, the killing and the drugs. The taxpayers are paying good money for protection and now the problem is so deeply entrenched, we can't keep up, so we go after the low hanging fruit, arresting kids and filling our court system and our prisons with minions."

Jay waited. If he could only fast forward through the whole bit, *just get through your damn diatribe, Pat.*

Pat stared at Jay. "Are you *listening* Jay, or are you just letting it go in one ear and out the other?"

"I'm listening."

"I'm serious. This is a problem for both of us."

"Okay, okay." Jay turned on the switch in his brain that helped him win elections. He knew how to focus on the needs of people. He could do a damn good job of listening when he was on. Pat knew him too well. He knew how to get Jay's attention.

"Jay, we need reform. I can't drive this issue, but you can."

"Wait a minute, Pat, I'm the one who needs the favor, remember? Besides, I've got bigger fish to fry with this gun problem."

"*Seriously?* Jay, we're talking about the same *thing.* We need to tackle this problem at its core. I think maybe we both need a favor here. I can provide the support to help regain the system that's worked for this country for over two hundred years, but I can't do it alone."

"What're you suggesting?"

"I'm saying we need to appeal to the people and then take it to Springfield."

"What Pat? You still haven't told me anything."

"We need to streamline our justice system. Somehow, we've got to prioritize what's most important to our people and to our city. Folks are *scared*, Jay. *We're* scared. Somebody has to stand up against the head of this monster rather than nibbling at its toes. It's a smokescreen. We're targeting the symptoms, trying to control what people do in the privacy of their own homes."

"Okay, Pat. I'm starting to get it now. You're wanting to come out of the closet, right?"

"Funny."

"Seriously, I knew you were gay the first time I met you. It's the *shoes*, Pat. You can always tell by the *shoes*."

"Stay with me, please."

"Okay, so how do we make this appeal to the people?"

"I think we need to loosen up on the morality issues so we can focus on criminal behavior. I think we can begin that process."

"I don't disagree with the first part, but I'm not following the second part."

"I think we should emphasize the responsibility of people to protect themselves. Take drugs for example."

"*Oh* no!" Jay shook his head.

"Please . . . hear me out Jay." Pat waited. Jay set his jaw. He'd heard it before.

"Go on . . . if you must."

"Here's the problem. We can't fight battles on every front. It's obvious that we've done little to control organized crime. Gangs are in our back yard, Jay. They're killing people every day to protect their territory. Guess what? This is *our* territory. We need to take it back."

"Organized crime is here to stay. You know and I know what will happen to this city if we take it head on."

"I think we both know what happened in the nineteen twenties."

"That was different."

"No. It's *not*. It's *exactly* the same. We've empowered the drug lords. Jay, we don't have a *gun* problem. We have an organized *crime* problem. Aside from the occasional lunatic, we see people gunned down every day in this city. It's not the *guns*. It's the *gangs* and their *leaders*."

Deep down, it made sense. But, it would never fly. People don't elect mayors who go against the moral grain.

"Jay. *Listen* to me. We can make a difference. But, we have no more room in our prisons. We have the highest incarceration rate in the world. Why? *Drugs*. The truth is, more people are killed by the guys protecting their drug territories in this country than the drugs themselves."

"This doesn't play well in the court of public opinion."

"I *know* that. But, I'm saying we can *change* that, if we take the time to show folks where the crime exists."

Jay shook his head. He'd been had. Pat knew what he wanted. Pat also knew what Jay wanted.

"Look, Pat, we can talk about this philosophical stuff until we're blue in the face. I'll think about what you said. In the meantime, I need time."

"I'll buy you some time, even though I think we're going in opposite directions here. *Think* about it, Jay. You don't want a police state as your legacy."

"That's not really what I want. I want order. I don't think we can give people carte blanche to engage in whatever they damn well please. But, I'll think about what you've said."

"Fair enough."

TOM AND GEORGE

"Hey George," Tom said.

"What?"

"Wonder what those two are talking about?"

George looked at the monitor. "Mayor Epstein and Attorney General Pat Thompson are two unlikely peas in a pod."

"Yeah."

Tom leaned back in his chair, away from the console, propping his feet and putting his hands behind his head. "What happened to Bernie?"

"Dunno." George dipped a sugar glazed donut into his coffee, leaned over and bit the moist end.

"I thought he'd lead them to Jack by now."

"Mmm hmm." George sipped his coffee. "If they don't find Jack, it's over."

TONY

The toilet flushed and Michael emerged. Tony imagined the old man surrounded by a brown cloud of olfactory insult.

"CNN's reporting isolated skirmishes around the country," Tony said.

"Who?" Michael asked. He plopped into the love seat, exhaling cigarette smoke, a welcome breathe of fresh air.

"Between gun supporters and gun control folks mostly. Nothing big."

"How'd you sleep cupcake?"

"I did okay, except for your snoring." Michael had slept on the bed. Tony on the floor.

Tony tilted his head. It hadn't hit him until that moment. "Where do ya live?"

"Around."

"What . . . are you *homeless* or something?"

"Nope. I live here."

"*Wait* a minute!"

"Not long. By my estimates, only about three more weeks."

"Shit."

"Am I messin' up your social calendar?"

"Dude. Look a*round*. This apartment's only two-hundred square feet at best. One room, not counting the RV sized bathroom."

"Lovely place."

"*Augh!*"

Michael stubbed his half finished cigarette into the plate. "You need me."

"Bernie's *dead*. I have a *job*. You have . . . I don't *know* what you have."

"I'll tell you everything you need to know."

"What?"

"You're not done."

Michael sat stone-faced, looking at an old Penthouse magazine resting on Tony's makeshift night stand. "We could do a little cleaning up around here."

"You're *kidding* me, right?"

No response. *What a piece of work, this guy.* "You can have the stuff in my trunk. I don't need it."

No response.

"You need money?"

"Nope. I don't have all day. We need to talk."

"About what?"

"About Bernie's boss."

"I don't know." Tony fidgeted on the love-seat. "I'm not sure I wanna meet this guy."

"You don't. But, you will."

"Not if I don't *want* to."

"Doesn't matter, you will," Michael said, his lips barely moving.

"Why *me*? Why not the *police*?"

"You gotta trust me."

"Look, I've been nice. But, I really need space. I'll help you find a place to live."

"I'll stay here. You'll want me around."

It was spooky, but Tony wondered maybe if he did need Michael. He'd give him a few days.

"Bill will have some information for us later today," Michael said.

"From the computers?"

"Yeah. You'll wanna see this."

BILL

Audio/video segments were stored as files in a nice retrievable system, each with a time and date. *Dorm Shower. Mayor's Office. Oak Park Elementary School. Home.* He'd been through a few of them. *Lib can go through them and the documents in detail when she wakes up.*

The other files were far more interesting to him. Bernie had elaborate drawings of his inventions along with special security software. The inventions were also catalogued into a neat filing system. *Hovercraft. Robot Spider. Mini-Submarine. Human Propelled Aircraft. Gun Turret. Mini Power Plant.*

The drawings were done to perfection, complete with bills of material. Bernie was probably an engineer or maybe a college professor in Romania, Bill surmised.

The plans for the mini submarine were intriguing. A bullet-shaped, injection-molded capsule could submerge to about fifty feet — judging by the length of hose wound around a reel located on the top rear deck. The hose had a float that would remain on the surface to provide air to the capsule, held taunt by a coil spring to retract the hose as it surfaced. A separate small tube with mouthpiece and check valve was located inside a bubble-shaped cockpit for exhaling carbon dioxide into the water. Like a recumbent bicycle, pedal power drove the front-mounted propellor and also pumped water in and out of a bladder for ballast. The small sub had an outside mounted torpedo tube through which — Bill had learned — Bernie wanted to sink the Odyssey in Lake Michigan. The Odyssey was a large party yacht.

The aircraft was also pedal powered, but had solar panels on the wings to provide an assist through a small dc motor connected to a lightweight band on plastic pulleys. The wings, struts, and tail were all helium-filled Mylar compartments designed to help provide additional lift while serving as structural components. Bill marveled at the design — which combined form and function — providing safety for the operator encapsulated in pressurized compartments as well as additional lift to help keep the craft airborne. Even the wind was used to spin a lightweight sail turbine, providing additional charge to a lithium air battery. Buoyancy was controlled using pedal power to displace helium with air or to compress air through a venturi, collecting condensate as ballast and drinking water, both released by a valve at the bottom of the bladder tank.

The file entitled Power Plant was encrypted. It would take some time to work through it, but if Bill knew anything, it was how to break security codes.

His computer made a noise. He looked at the monitor to his side. An instant message had popped up.

"*I'd like to speak with you about a possible job.*"

He didn't recognize the user, *D2*.

He tapped his response.

"*I would like to hear more.*"

He waited.

"*Meet my assistant at the Trump Tower Entrance on Monday at noon. I'll buy you lunch.*"

His pulse quickened. *Who is it?* His first instinct was to ask questions, yet, it seemed risky to question such an offer.

But, how would they meet?

He tapped the keys. "*Okay . . . ?*"

A few seconds passed.

"*LOL! Don't worry. We'll find you.*"

Lib stretched on the floor. Rex stood up and licked her on the face. "Hey Rexy," she said, scratching his ears.

"I got everything running. It took a few hours, but I managed to get through a few simple pass codes, gaining access to most of the files."

"Great." Lib yawned.

"Can I get you something to eat?"

"Not right now. I had horrible dreams."

"I know. I heard you."

She sat on her folded legs with her head on his thigh and arms around his waist as he sat in the chair. Warm air permeated the fabric of his pants where she lay, hair tousled around her face.

"Can we take off all our clothes and just snuggle together in your bed?" she murmured into his leg.

Bill thought for a second. He liked the drawings and wanted to find out more. Yet, somehow, the drawings could wait.

"Yes."

"I thought so."

LIB

The bedroom furniture had been passed down from his grandparents, she'd discovered, as they lay under the covers — skin pressed together. She needed intimacy.

She couldn't help thinking about Bernie. No matter what he'd done, he was still a human being. He'd probably suffered more than she'd ever know. She'd ended his life, delivering the final blow to whatever injustice he'd felt. What could she have done differently?

Somehow, lying naked beside Bill gave her comfort. She felt the warmth of his body radiating into her, reminding her that she remained part of the human race. Bill was her anchor, letting her know she was not alone and that someone would accept her — look beyond her transgressions.

As a girl, her comfort came from her parents and the animals on the farm. They were there for her, no matter what. Since moving to Chicago, she'd been alone except for a few crappy relationships. She hadn't received the warmth she needed. She needed to feel part of something — something she could count on at the end of the day after enduring all the troubles of the world. Bill delivered it to her in the most unimaginable way. He was just there, gently talking when she wanted to talk. Oddly, she no longer feared silence. It was not awkward to listen to the sounds of the world outside of their window together — sometimes for fifteen minutes without saying a word. They spoke through their skin. It was the most wonderful feeling to lie together — free from the world, free from the burden to fill the air with needless chatter, free from the expectation of sex, free from the inhibition of society.

"I don't want you to take this the wrong way," she spoke into his chest. "I mean . . . " It was too soon. She'd almost said it. *No. Say something else.* " . . . just getting naked and laying together . . . I like it."

"Me too."

"Can we just walk around naked all day."

"It's okay with me."

Lib heard a blue jay screeching outside. "I'm not kidding."

"Can I tell you something strange?" he said.

"Of course."

"I feel closer to you when we're naked."

"We are closer, silly."

"No, I mean . . . emotionally."

She ran her finger along his chest. Yes. She did love this man. He was on the same wavelength.

"Let's go raid the refrigerator, naked as blue jays," she said.

"Okay."

Lib threw the covers back, and stood on the bed, jumping up and down, her breasts moving counter to her body as Bill smiled his approval. He stood up with her, jumping up and down — his penis stiff and flopping up and down. They were adult children! She jumped from the bed and ran. She heard him following her so she ran around the apartment — up on the couch — Rex barking and wagging his tail — into the kitchen and to the refrigerator where they both stood, breathing hard.

Bill pulled out a block of cheddar cheese and a few Diet

Cokes and set them on the counter. Leaning into the fridge, he found a bunch of green seedless grapes in the drawer. *Nice*.

He placed the cheese and grapes on a plate retrieved from the cabinet and they walked into the office, sitting cross-legged on the carpet — devouring their find, nourishing their naked bodies.

"I can't believe I'm hanging out with a com*put*er hacker."

He stood and sat at the desk. "An ex-computer hacker."

"What about *my* computer? Can you get in?"

"Your computer wasn't connected to an internet service provider, so, no. But, these days, it's not that difficult, except guys like Bernie who can set up elaborate firewalls."

Bill showed her Bernie's files as she leaned over his shoulder — her breasts barely touching his skin, her nipples hard with excitement. They would make wild, passionate love later, but for the moment she was having fun. She sat on his leg for a few minutes, sliding around and giggling.

She took over his place at the computer and read a few files as he stood next to her.

TONY

"So cupcake, what do you suppose they're doin' right now?"

"Who?"

"Your girlfriend and the computer kid."

Tony glared at him.

"C'mon cupcake. It's not the end of the world."

"Yesterday you were talking about *mortality*, now *this*. What can I *say*?"

"I'm trying to help you through it."

"Thanks. That's kinda like helping someone dying of thirst by dragging them through the desert, wouldn't you say?"

"What's that word? Oh. Cathodic. It's cathodic."

"Cathartic." Tony shook his head. "Cathodic means negatively charged electrode."

"You're a smart guy. Why can't you find a nice girl to ride you into the sunset?"

"Damn. You're some kinda sensitive, you know that?"

"Enough happy chitchat. We need a plan."

Tony sighed. He didn't want to play this game anymore, but Michael knew something. "What *kind* of plan?"

"You need to study Bernie's boss like you studied for exams at Columbia."

"Seriously?"

"Yeah. You're probably right. Maybe you should study

this guy much harder than you studied at Columbia."

"You have no idea how hard I worked to get through school."

"You had a 2.67 GPA, cupcake.   That ain't exactly Pulitzer Prize material now, is it?"

Tony sighed again.

"Here's the deal.   Information is your friend.   You'll need it later."

"Why do you keep talking about the future like that? You said you'd be here three weeks. Now, you're telling me I'll need information like I'm fulfilling some kind of destiny or something. You need to fess up."

"You're not ready for the truth, Tony."

"The truth is stranger than fiction, so just give it to me."

"In due time. In due time.

BILL

They'd explored every inch of his apartment. The office. The kitchen. The dining room. The bathroom. Teasing and alternating between ordinary daylight activities and things that he'd never heard of before. He'd been introduced to a new world.

Lib sat again at the computer. Still naked but not as playful. She seemed fixed on one particular document.

"What is it?" he asked.

She sat straight with her back gently arched — a scene out of his dreams — a beautiful naked woman sitting at a computer. She squirmed a bit in the chair. He could see her dark mound blending with the black naugahyde seat — her legs on either side.

"This guy is really bad. I mean, he's into everything."

"What?"

"He's into drugs. He's into prostitution. He's into investments and government corruption. He's the money guy, paying for protection, but they have no idea where he comes from."

"I am confused."

"It says here that he may be the American implant for the Los Diablos cartel in Mexico. But, nobody knows where he's located. They know of his existence only through intercepted communications with drug lords and, of course, through our friend Bernie."

149

"I know something about the drugs. One division of NSA is involved."

"He has ties to our government, using money to gain inside information to help his key people."

"I think it is sad when our government is involved."

"Yeah, me too. It's absurd. I think it's only the tip of the iceberg."

"Why don't we arrest them?"

"I love your innocence." She turned and smiled. "Okay, so you're not that innocent anymore, but it's not that easy. These folks are very dangerous and very deeply entrenched. A lot of people get killed."

"How can these things happen in a civilized country?"

"Good question. Ask your Congressman."

Bill had worked to control international terrorism. This sounded a lot like domestic terrorists. How many millions are spent to help other countries? *Why can we not do something to help ourselves*?

"I think I will."

"What?"

"Ask my Congressman."

"Ha, ha, ha. You do that." Lib continued to read, scanning some of the files. "What are these?"

"Oh. Bernie designed some very interesting machines. Let me show you."

Lib stood and Bill sat on the moist seat. He pulled up the submarine design, rolling the chair back so she could see. She leaned over and inspected the drawing, her breasts dangling.

"Oh my *God*! That's so *cool*!"

He showed her the aircraft and the blimp and the spider.

"I get excited about technology. What's *this*?" She pointed to the file entitled *Power Plant*.

"That file is encrypted. I can probably decode it, but it might take a while."

"Maybe it's worth money."

"If it is what I think, then yes, it's probably worth some money. So are these other designs."

"What if we could sell them?" Lib looked at him, biting her lip. "Oh wait. You probably wouldn't want to steal someone else's ideas to make money."

"I have Asperger's. I am not crazy. Bernie is dead. He killed a lot of people. If we can make money, then we will give some to the families of the victims."

"I think I love you."

Bill felt the blood rushing into his extremities. "I think I love you, too."

TONY

"I have a solution," Michael said.

"A solution for what?"

"A solution for our living arrangement here."

Michael sat on the bed, dipping Cheetos into peanut butter.

"Hey, you think maybe you could stop spreading *Cheetos* dust on my sheets? *Jeez.*"

"Sorry. It's a bad habit."

"So what's your solution?"

"I've been thinking. You were right, it's a small place and we're two grown men. I think we should give each other some space."

"*Now* you're talking."

"Why don't you move over to Lib's apartment."

"*What*?"

"She's probably not using it now."

"Aw, c'mon dude!"

"Really. I'll bet her feet are high in the air, giving spy boy a ride through Lib canyon. Her place is emptier than your social calendar right about now."

"*Ouch*!"

"See how that works? The stark reality of your desolate condition is easier once you've faced it straight on."

"You know, you don't have to candy coat it on account of me."

"Well, anyway, I thought you might need a little time to

yourself. A place you can call your own."

"This *is* my place."

"Well, it's kinda crowded with us *both* here, ain't it?"

"You're not only *mean*, you're *nasty*! Look at my *bed*!"

"See what I mean? You're all worked up. You need some space, cupcake."

* * *

Tony'd left Michael at the apartment. He would've given him a key but it seemed as though he really didn't need one.

He'd called Lib. She sounded good. Maybe Michael was right. Maybe having it rubbed in his face was liberating. It was cathartic. Determined to move on, he'd go to Bill's apartment and he'd hang out with them and smile, demonstrating his "moving-on-ness." If he needed reality to slap him in the face, this would do it.

He checked himself, smiling in the rearview mirror briefly while driving to Bill's apartment. Resolving his mission, he prepared himself emotionally for the experience, visualizing the image that Michael'd already created for him. He imagined them in every position, speeding up the motion in his mind and slowing it down just for fun, like a TV remote control.

He was good. He could stand on his own two feet, go in there and get the information he needed, and then ask Lib for the key to her apartment. Why? Because he was over it. A grown man. Maybe he'd become their downstairs neighbor friend.

LIB

The doorbell rang. She'd put on one of Bill's button down shirts and a pair of his gym shorts, her hair still wet from showering together with Bill.

Tony's head seemed unusually large through the peep hole. She'd never seen him quite this way before, like a man in a gravity chamber, the magnified weight of the world tugging at the skin on his face.

Opening the door, she smiled and welcomed him in.

"Yeah. Thanks," he said, eyes scanning her choice of attire. "I need the key to your apartment, a place to hang out for a while."

"Uh, yeah, sure. I'll grab an extra chair." Tony seemed anxious, yet his shoulders were slumped to match his face — like a dog beaten by his master.

"Bill will be out in a minute. He's brushing his teeth." Lib immediately regretted referring to Bill like a roommate or husband.

"So . . . I . . . how're you guys doing?" Tony tried to smile. It looked more like a grimace.

"Oh, we're good." *Damn*! She'd referred to herself and Bill as "we." She couldn't stop herself.

Tony sat and looked around the room at the computer equipment, his hands on his knees, drumming his fingers. "Nice stuff."

Lib edited her phrases before speaking. "Yes, Bill likes

to work in here on his computer."

Damn! She thought. *Now I sound like I've been here for a month*!

Bill walked in. "Hello, Tony. Nice to see you again." Tony shook his hand, perhaps a little too hard judging by the expression on Bill's face.

Bill leaned over and kissed Lib on the cheek. She darted her eyes from right to left a few times to remind Bill that Tony was in the room with them. Bill seemed a little confused, but sat down near the computer.

"So, what did you find out?" Tony asked.

"A lot of information about Bernie's boss," Lib offered before Bill could speak. She was fearful of what he might say. He didn't know about Tony.

"Also, Bernie designed some interesting machines," Bill said. "I'll show you if you want to see them."

Tony slapped his knees and then stretched his arms straight out in front of him. "Well, this has been really nice. I guess I should run along. Got a date tonight with a nice pediatrician I met at a big fundraiser last week. Dr. Quinn."

"No, no! *Please* don't leave!" Lib said.

Bill looked at Lib, taking her cue. "No, you should stay for dinner. Lib makes really good lasagna."

Lib widened her eyes at Bill. He winked at her, perhaps further acknowledging his misunderstanding. "Tony. I am so impressed with Lib. She is teaching me so much."

Lib rolled her eyes. *Oh well*.

"Okay. *Enough*. I give *up*," Tony said.

Bill said, "Excuse me?" a puzzled look on his face.

"I came over to get the key to Lib's apartment, *Finkle*-Roy. I'd love to hang around and *chat* with you lovebirds, but I'm gonna go downstairs and put my *head* in the oven."

"My name is Bill."

Lib quickly shook her head from side to side at Bill who creased his forehead.

"Tony.　Please, just wait a minute.　I think we're all friends," she said.

"Friends?"　Bill looked directly at Lib with puppy dog eyes. "But you said you *loved* me."

"Darling, I *do* love you, but we're trying to reach out to *Tony* right now, okay?"

"Oh pul*lease*!　Just get me a bottle of sleeping pills and a bottle of whisky, *will* ya?" Tony whined.

"Why are we reaching out to Tony?"

"Because he's in *pain*, *DEAR*."　She tilted her head to one side, eyes wide and eyebrows raised, trying to break through.

"Why is Tony in pain?"

"Just kill me now."

"*Wait* a minute!　Everybody *stop*!!!!" Lib shouted.

She couldn't take it anymore.　"Tony.　Please don't leave.　You're gonna be fine."

She looked at Bill. "Bill."

"Yes?"

"Tony has a crush on me but he knows that we'll never be together, especially since I'm sitting in your clothes and cooking your favorite lasagna for dinner.　It makes him very sad."

Tony had slumped down in the chair, head resting on the back, arms drooping to both sides.　He looked at the ceiling with unblinking wide eyes.

"Ohhh," Bill responded.

"And Bill."

"Yes."

"We have to be extra nice to Tony right now."

"I get it now.　So he won't stick his head in the oven,

right?"

"Right."

"Okay, your turn, Bill. I need to be honest here."

"Tony?"

"What?"

"Bill has Asperger's. He doesn't always get subtle communications. He wasn't trying to be mean to you, he just didn't catch on."

Tony looked at Bill then at Lib. "Are you *kidding* me? You're schtupping an *Aspie*?"

"What is schtupping?"

Lib put her hand on Bill's leg. "Bill, hold on a minute, please." She looked at Tony. "He's a *person*, Tony, just like you and me. We all have our flaws. I'm a Libertarian who abhors injustice and overreaching government. You, Tony, are an insolent boor with no friends. Rex? Rex is just a dog with no balls. So, let's enjoy each other's company in all our imperfection."

"Seriously?"

"Seriously. We're gonna march into the other room and say nice things to each other and pretend this conversation never happened. Bill?"

"Okay."

"Tony."

"Okay. But I was serious about the key to your apartment. Michael's taken up residence at my place."

"No problem."

* * *

"You awake?"

"Yes." Bill responded. "I can't sleep."

"What's wrong?"

"I had a bad dream."

"Yeah, me too."

Lib slid closer to him, feeling the warmth of his body. "You tell me yours and I'll tell you mine." She waited for Bill to process. *One Mississippi, two Mississippi, three Mississippi . . .*

"I dreamed I was back in grad school, except I saw a few folks from NSA there. At one point, I'm sitting at a lunch table alone. Guys are sitting all around at the other tables and one character with long hair and a beard is chiding me about sitting by myself, making me look like an idiot. I felt the sting of his verbal attacks, but it was so embarrassing, I felt even more alone than before. Then, I'm in a locker room, seeing rows of nice maple stained lockers for the very first time. I hadn't yet received a locker, so one of the guys offered an empty one to me. They were all undressing to go into a men's shower. I froze. I didn't want to be in the men's shower with a bunch of naked men."

Lib waited, thinking about Bill's dream. "That's it?"

"Yes."

"That's not so bad."

"It is for *me*."

She thought about it again. *Is he gay? Well, duh. Bisexual? Why would a bisexual man fear being in a shower with a bunch of naked men?* Maybe it was Bill's fear of exposure. He didn't want to be naked. He was alone. The shower was communal. Maybe, for Bill, being part of a community was embarrassing. It made sense, but she wouldn't offer her analysis to him. She just patted his hand for reassurance.

"What about your dream?" Bill asked.

"It's absurd."

"So was mine."

"Okay." She thought about it for a few seconds,

composing her thoughts. "I'm with a friend . . . we're adults, but we're in my bedroom at my home in Indiana. My girlfriend is sleeping over. My father walks in with a bong."

"What's a bong?"

"It's a pipe that people use to smoke marijuana and hashish. It has water in it to cool the smoke." Lib couldn't believe Bill didn't know about a bong. "Anyway, so my friend says, 'It's mine,' and my dad walks over and sets the water pipe down with a bunch of other drug paraphernalia. It's so weird. It's not like my father at all. He wasn't like that. He would've called the police."

"Have you smoked marijuana?"

"Yes. Have you?"

"No."

"Do you still smoke it?"

"No."

"Good."

"I had another dream," Lib continued. "I dreamed I was on a train. I'd written an article about gangs in Chicago and a man with a bandana stood next to me. I was uncomfortable. He just stared at me, so I looked away at the strange collection of people, most of whom I knew, standing around. It was my stop, so I stepped toward the door. The man with the bandana followed me out. I looked at him. He pointed his finger like a gun and said 'BANG, you're dead.'"

"That is scary."

"Yeah, *tell* me about it."

She caressed his arm as they lay together, side by side.

"Are you okay?" Bill asked softly.

"Yeah."

"I mean about Bernie."

"Oh. Yeah. I guess." She'd tried not thinking about it, but it tugged at her conscience. "Am I going to hell?"

"No."

"What makes you so sure?"

"You have a heart, and a soul. I can feel it."

Bill's hand was on her breast. "Uh, Bill. That's not my soul."

"We cannot possibly follow the law to perfection."

"I *killed* him. I shot Bernie in his own *house*. That's not a misdemeanor offense."

Bill nuzzled her ear, kissing her lobe. "I am not talking about our laws," he said softly, "I'm talking about God's laws. That's why we have grace."

It was an interesting parallel to her, though she wasn't in the mood to talk about theology. "Maybe you're right. Maybe it's the same struggle in society between order and liberty."

She waited for his response. "Bill?" He was asleep.

BILL

Busy men and women rotated in and out of the revolving door at the Wabash entrance to Trump Tower, creating a *kawhooshing* noise. The tonality and pitch of the sound fascinated Bill. He emulated the noise, unintentionally drawing the eyes of a woman walking past, then reminded himself not to make strange noises in public.

"Bill Tee?" He turned toward the voice — a man wearing a tan suit.

Remember to look him in the eyes, Lib had reminded him before he left. He extended his hand and smiled, looking directly at the man's nose. It was close enough.

"Ron Jepson," he said, shaking Bill's hand.

"It is very nice to meet you," Bill said.

"Let's go upstairs to Mr. Dickens' office."

Mr. Jepson entered the revolving door. Bill stepped into the next compartment and walked in time with the door, then stepped inside the lobby of the fabulous hotel, admiring the dark brown zebra wood on the surrounding walls.

"Very nice building."

The man smiled at him.

Mr. Jepson led them to an elevator requiring a special key. The pocket doors opened to a large compartment with mirrored walls.

"Mr. Trump must like to see himself in the mirrors."

"I believe maybe you're right."

The pressure changed rapidly. Mr. Jepson stretched his mouth into a yawn as a small screen displayed ads for Sixteen restaurant and the downstairs spa.

"Where are the lights?"

"This elevator only makes two stops."

Bing. The doors opened.

DICKENS AND ASSOCIATES was mounted in large aluminum letters high on a stained mahogany wood wall surrounding a large opening directly in front of the elevator. They walked through the opening to a large reception area where a woman sat behind a desk on the left side wearing a dark suit. She pressed a button, unlocking a glass double door to a room on their right, paneled in the same reddish wood. "Please sit," Jepson said.

The soft leather groaned as the cushions of the wing chair formed around his body.

"Mr. Dickens will be with you in a minute." Jepson walked back through the glass doors, turning to the right at the receptionist's desk, and then down the hall.

A large portrait of a man sitting in a similar leather wing chair hung on the end wall, highlighted by a brass lamp. The man's face was tanned and deeply wrinkled like an old Hollywood actor. He smiled, but his eyes were not smiling. His penetrating gaze intimidated Bill. The man in the painting wore a dark suit, light blue shirt and a red tie, matching a large ruby ring on his pinky. His hands rested on the arms of the chair.

"Some people say I look cold," a voice said from behind the chair. Bill stood and noticed a wrinkled forehead belonging to the same man from the painting. He was similarly dressed, except with a gold tie. Bill extended his hand and smiled. The man calmly took Bill's hand and shook slowly but firmly.

A scar extended the length of Mr. Dickens' right eyebrow, becoming Bill's focal point.

"Unfortunate accident. I slipped on the deck of a ship during a storm and hit my head on a capstan."

"Sorry, I . . . "

"No need to explain. Ich verstehen."

"You speak German."

"I also speak French, Spanish, Dutch and Mandarin."

"I am still struggling with English."

Mr. Dickens laughed. "I like your honesty. Please join me for lunch."

They walked straight across, past the receptionist through wooden double doors into a private dining room with large glass windows overlooking the Chicago River. Bill could see Marina City, the iconic apartment buildings resembling two ears of corn — their balconies highlighted by the midday sun.

A single table near the window was set for two. They sat as a stream of wait staff brought glasses of water, a basket of bread, and a dish of something that looked like potted meat.

"What kind of food is this?"

"It's pate de foie gras." Dickens cut a slice of bread and spread a generous portion of pate before taking a bite. Bill did the same. It tasted much better than potted meat.

"This food is delicious."

"It's fattened goose liver."

"Oh."

It did not taste like liver.

"What would you like for your lunch?"

"What do they serve here?"

Dickens laughed. "They'll prepare anything you want."

"I'll have a peanut butter and jelly sandwich and a glass

of milk."

"As you wish. *Waiter*!"

Within seconds, a man wearing a tuxedo stood next to Mr. Dickens.

"My new friend would like a peanut butter and jelly sandwich, prepared with the finest fresh peanuts from Georgia. Oh, and a glass of milk. I'll have my usual."

A large boat with tourists floated under a bridge six hundred feet below them, green water shimmering in the sunlight.

"I heard you're looking for a new job."

"Yes, but how did you know?"

Dickens smiled. Bill could feel his eyes, but he dared not look into them.

"It's part of my business to know when high level people are interested in an opportunity of a lifetime."

Like many expressions, "opportunity of a lifetime" confused Bill. How does Mr. Dickens know it is the opportunity of a lifetime? Opportunity has different meanings to different people. "How can I help you?" Bill asked.

"You see, not everyone asks how they may help me. They always want to know how I will help them. I see your potential, perhaps more than you see in yourself."

Bill shifted in his seat. It was nice that someone so important would take an interest in him. He wanted to know more, but forced himself to wait rather than risk saying something wrong, like how do you define opportunity of a lifetime?

"I need someone like you, Bill. I need your experience decoding encrypted messages and . . . well . . . getting past firewalls."

The waiter pushed a cart to the table. He placed sterling

silver covered dishes in front of both men then poured a glass of red wine for Mr. Dickens followed by a glass of milk for Bill.

The waiter then removed the domed covers, revealing Bill's quartered peanut butter and jelly sandwich on plain white bread surrounding a red julienned vegetable in the center. On Dickens' plate, a roast duckling with the same vegetable. "Bon appetite!"

Mr. Dickens raised his wine glass. "To a successful partnership."

Bill lifted his milk. They clinked their glasses together.

The peanut butter wasn't like Jiff or Peter Pan. It was savory, like meat. The jelly tasted like cranberries and the bread was warm, fresh out of the oven.

"After lunch, we'll visit your new office and you'll meet your personal assistant."

"What does a personal assistant do?"

"Whatever you ask." Dickens smiled.

Bill finished his sandwich then watched the older man skillfully dissect the whole duck with surgical precision.

A creaking sound drew Bill's attention to the doors through which they'd entered. A man in an expensive suit walked toward them, smiling.

"Bill, I'd like you to meet Gerard leBanquier, my Director of Investment Operations."

The man extended his hand. "Bonjour."

"Nice to meet you," Bill said, shaking his hand.

"If you accept my offer, you will work closely with Gerard, helping to capitalize on investment opportunities based on our research."

"That sounds interesting."

Gerard smiled and spoke with a French lilt. "We are on the cutting edge of technolo-jee, able to manage our assets based on real time data."

The waiter returned with three small glasses and a bottle. He placed the glasses down and filled each with a brown liquid.

Gerard raised his glass. "À succès." Dirk and Bill stood, clinking their glasses.

Dirk extended his hand toward Bill, palm up, gesturing. "Drink it. It's cognac."

Bill tasted the drink. It was strong, like cough syrup.

"It's Remy Martin, Louis XIII."

"It sounds expensive."

"It does sound expensive, doesn't it?"

"Yes."

Bill sipped the cognac, watching seagulls hover around a crowd of tourists waiting to board a charter boat.

"It's time to go."

The three men walked back out to the reception area together.

The receptionist sat, hands folded in front of her as though posing for a photograph. "This is Wanda." She smiled and waved as they turned right, walking through a set of glass double doors into an office area with cubicles on one side and glassed offices on the other. Dickens pointed to the side where twenty or thirty people sat in cubicles. Some talked on telephones. "These people work for me."

"What are they doing?"

"A lot of things. For example, they provide emotional and psychological support to those who need a friend." Mr. Dickens said.

"I don't understand."

"We help people who are depressed and angry. They're like wounded animals who need our care."

"How do you make money helping people?"

"That's a very good question, my honest and open friend. Money's not a problem here."

Gerard excused himself. Dickens pointed to the other side, a row of glassed offices, one through which Mr. leBanquier entered and sat at his computer.

"This is Investment Operations." Dickens pointed to a large screen with market data scrolling. "We're primarily focused on futures and options, mostly currencies. Come with me."

Bill followed Dickens to a larger office, following him through a glass door to the exterior glass wall with a view of Lake Michigan. Behind them, Bill could see the elevators through the opposite glass partition wall through which they'd entered. "Good afternoon, Mr. Dickens." A woman with blonde hair pulled back into a ponytail stood near two ficus trees in a modest gray suit, her hands folded behind her back.

"Good afternoon, Cherise." Dickens handed a key card to Bill. "This is your new office, assuming that you'll join us."

Four large computer monitors sat side by side on a credenza against the glass exterior wall. Between them and the credenza, a large open style desk and office chair sat waiting.

"What would you like for me to do?"

"I want you to do what you do best. I want you to collect information."

Mr. Dickens handed Bill a silver key on a keyring. "But first, I want you to go with Cherise. I'll talk to you later."

The key had the image of a black horse, the familiar trademark for the Italian carmaker, Ferrari.

Mr. Dickens walked out of the office.

"Hello," Cherise said.

"Hello.   I am Bill Tee," he said, looking at her mouth. "Where are we going?"

"We're going shopping, Bill Tee," Cherise said.

TOM AND GEORGE

"There he is," George said.

They both leaned forward, peering at the monitor on the console — an image of Bill and Cherise walking through the lobby of the Trump Tower.

Tom shook his head. "I don't like it. Maybe we should call the boss."

"I'm sure the boss knows what's going on."

The chair squeaked as Tom leaned back. "Yeah, I guess you're right. Pass me the Crunch and Munch will ya?"

LIB

She looked at the blinking lights on a router Bill had installed, providing Tony access to Bernie's files. Tony was downstairs in her apartment, now with a dining room table and a few chairs borrowed from Bill.

Rex rested his chin on her bare foot as she typed. The previous two days had given her time to collect her thoughts after so many things had happened. Bill was there for her. He seemed to know that she needed his warmth to help her push the guilt and sorrow aside. Now wasn't the time to feel sorry for Bernie. In a way, she'd helped him, but she, along with her co-conspirators had collectively taken the law into their hands.

She tapped a few keys, pulling up ChicagoTribune.com and stared at the top story for the day. *SHOOTINGS CONTINUE DESPITE CITYWIDE GUN BAN.* *What shootings? What ban?* She read the article. Several kids were killed in Brookhaven, the area known for drug traffic in which gangs regularly shot each other, protecting their territory. It didn't make it any easier, but it was the status quo. She'd almost accepted it. It was far better to cope with senseless tragedies than to drive herself into therapy, worrying about kids doomed from the start, not having the means to help themselves out of the economic desolation of Brookhaven.

Lib had approached John, her editor, about exposing

organized crime. "It's not a good assignment for you," he'd said. He protected her, not only from the dark corners of society, but also from the risk of being targeted. It scared her to think about it. If everybody is scared, then it'll never change, she'd argued. It'd gotten her nowhere.

She thought about the potential for exposing the Los Diablos drug cartel. Maybe she could convince John that a larger perspective might draw more attention to the root cause of gun violence in all cities around the country, not just Chicago.

She read another article. Someone shot two tourists from a distance at Navy Pier. They had no suspects, but the weapon was a Mini 14. *Was it copycats*? Bernie was dead. They'd found remaining pieces of the sawed up Mini 14 in his basement. *What was going on*?

In national news, a student had walked into a school, killing four classmates and the teacher before killing himself. *Why? Why does a kid do this sort of thing? Was it bullying? Was this a response to a world gone mad?*

She called the Illinois State Government Offices across from Daley Center.

"Pat Thompson's office please."

A woman answered the phone, "Attorney General's Office."

"I'm an old friend of Pat Thompson. I'd like to speak with him."

"Mr. Thompson's a busy man."

"Please, just tell him it's Lib Rand." She waited as music from hell kept her company, reminding her of the likelihood that Pat would never know she called. *How long could anyone listen to sterile, computer-generated music? Absurd*!"

The music stopped. "Pat Thompson."

"Hi Pat. It's Lib."

"Holy *cow*! Lib, how *are* you?"

"I'm good. I'm at the *Trib* now."

"I know. I've seen a few of your pieces. Still trying to change the world."

She laughed. They'd met at a Libertarian rally in Cambridge — became friends her junior year — he was a senior. "That makes *two* of us."

"How can I help you?"

"I'd like to buy you coffee."

"Nobody buys me coffee unless they want something." He laughed.

"I have an idea for a piece on gun violence. I'd like your perspective."

"I have a better idea. Let me buy you lunch."

"Today?"

"Yeah. You busy?"

Lib hesitated. *Was he hitting on her*? They'd had a moment in college, but ended up friends for the most part.

"No."

"Don't worry, it's just two friends catching up on old times and sharing idealistic dreams like the old days."

"Okay. What time and where?"

"Meet me at The Little Goat on W. Randolph at 11:30."

"Will do."

TONY

More shootings. *Maybe I'll become a monk*, Tony thought. His life was no longer in his control. He'd witnessed a horrific murder and a bomb exploding at Daley Plaza on television. He'd been threatened by a lunatic with a pistol before a mist of blood ruined his favorite button down. He'd allowed another lunatic to live in his apartment, soiling his sheets with God knows what. Meanwhile, Lib preferred a computer geek with no common sense. As a further reminder of his despair, Lib, in a moment of undying compassion had arranged for him to sleep in the room directly below Bill's bedroom. Chicago was under attack. The Cubs were swept by the Braves. At the moment, being a monk didn't seem so bad.

"*You're not alone*," an instant message popped up with the id, *LUV*.

Tony tapped his reply. "*Who is this?*"

A few seconds passed.

"*A friend who cares.*"

Who could it be?

"*If you care so much, why are you hiding?*"

Maybe it was enough to discourage an anonymous interloper. Probably some kid.

"*You need me. I'll show you.*"

"*How?*"

His phone rang. Facetime. *Who's Lena?*, he wondered.

He pressed a button and a young woman in a sweatshirt with light reddish hair appeared. She wore a Bluetooth. *"Hi Tony."*

"Hi. Is this some kind of live porn service?"

She smiled. *"Well, not exactly."*

"Damn. Then what exactly?"

"I just want you to know I'm here for you."

She sipped a cup of coffee.

"Show me your boobies."

She looked to either side, sat her coffee down out of view of the camera, then lifted her sweatshirt and bra, quickly revealing smallish breasts with small, strawberry colored nipples before arranging her clothing back into place.

"You need a credit card number?"

"No. I just want you to trust me. I'm reaching out to you."

"You'll do anything I ask?"

"No. That's not what you need right now."

He shook his head. It didn't add up, yet the truth is sometimes stranger than fiction.

"How do you know what I need?"

"I just do. You're in pain. You need a friend."

Weird though it seemed, especially from a total stranger, she was right. Having a pretty woman as a potential friend on Facetime was nice, but the thought that someone knew his pain was oddly comforting and unsettling at the same time.

She sat calmly, sipping her coffee again. *What's with this chick?*

"Is Lena your real name?"

"Yes."

"Can you tell me your last name?"

"*Not right now.*"

"What do you do?"

She smiled again. Nice teeth.

"*I'm doing it now. Can we talk again later?*"

"Sure."

"*Bye.*" Icons for his apps appeared on his phone. She was gone.

It was enough encouragement to draw him out of his doldrums for a moment or two. He needed to do something. It was the best way to deal with loneliness. He selected an icon on his computer and perused Bernie's files.

Bill had already determined the password for most of the text documents. The larger file contained a journal, Bill had said.

Tony opened Bernie's journal, reading about Bernie's anger and frustration and lonliness. He shivered at the man's insanity, reading his innermost thoughts and desires. Bernie was a raving lunatic, bent on paying the world back for his pain. Tony continued to read. Midway through the journal, Bernie's attitude seems to change. He stopped complaining about his security job. He seemed cheerful.

. . . I have money in checking. Jack says I'm good for business, sends money from Thailand. I keep working hard, maybe get cocaine and girls, have big party. . .

Tony read the last entry written on the day of the bombing.

. . . Big shipment. Create diversion.

Tony heard a noise behind him.

"Whatcha thinkin' 'bout cupcake?"

"*Jeez*!!"

Michael sat on the floor in the corner of the room. "Really love what you've done with the place."

"Yeah, it's wonderful. How'd *you* get in here?"

Michael lit a cigarette. He wore the same clothes. "Terrible about those tourists."

"Well, the world is crazy. What else is new?"

"If you'd stop focusing on yourself, you might find the answer is closer than you think."

"Gimme a *break*."

"It's time to let go of your fear." Michael thumped an ash into his hand.

Tony turned in his chair, facing him. "Okay. I've about *had* it. Who the hell do you think you *are*?"

"I think you know."

"Why would I ask?"

Michael licked his fingers and pressed them against the lit end of the cigarette, then put the extinguished cigarette into his shirt pocket.

"I'm a guardian angel," he said with the same deadpan, gravelly voice. He sat stone faced in the corner of the room, his arm dangling on one raised knee.

"That's just *great*, Michael. Who put you *up* to this?"

No response.

"I don't know what you're up to, but it's gone too far."

No response.

"Well, you don't look like a guardian angel to me."

"Ever seen one before?"

"Can't say that I have."

"Well, there ya go."

"Are you sure you're not from the *other* place?"

"Yep."

"*Prove* it."

Michael scratched his head. "You grew up Catholic."

"So?"

"But, you left the church. It happens to a lot of folks."

Tony rolled his eyes.

Michael raised his dangling arm and pointed a bony finger at him. "Good times are easy, but it's also easy to lose our way when things get tough."

"Thank you once again for your platitudes."

"You just don't want to scratch below the surface, do you? When things go wrong, you're just like most folks who give up and go the other way. Just a little suffering and —BAM! — off you go into the deep end of the pool."

"You know what? You've got a lotta nerve. Yeah. Things aren't great. Maybe I need someone to help get me back on track. What do *I* get? I get *you*!"

"Feeling sorry for yourself ain't gonna fix it. Your just holdin' a sign that says, 'Come and get me devil.'"

Tony sighed. "What does God look like?"

"You don't believe in him. It's easier for you."

Tony pressed his lips together. "I didn't say that."

"Yeah, but you think it."

"What's heaven like?"

Michael screwed his pinky into his ear, and then inspected it before wiping it on his pants. "It's actually a lot of fun. Free beer. You can drink it all day — every day — and never gain weight or get sick."

"Yeah, *right*."

"Cheeseburgers for breakfast."

"I have that now."

"You can eat as long and as much as you can put into your mouth, but you don't have to eat at all if you don't want."

Tony smirked.

"The Cubs win the World Series."

"When?"

"Every day, if you want."

Tony faked a smile. "What about my mom and dad?"

"Your mom's doing great, cupcake."

"So, who told you?"

"What?"

"Who told you my mom called me cupcake?"

"She did."

"Okay . . . so . . . *why* did she call me that?"

Michael used the wall to lift himself, shaking one leg after standing. "You ate a whole pan of cupcakes the day before your 9th birthday. It made you sick."

Tony's lip quivered. "You're some kinda guardian angel. I'm down here sufferin' and you're tryin' to drive a *nail* in my coffin!"

Michael shook his head slowly. "What did I tell you about feelin' sorry for yourself? Besides, I never said I was *your* guardian angel."

Tony turned back to the computer, trying to ignore the old man. Struggling to focus, Tony spoke. "You're a huge distraction." No answer. Tony turned around. Michael was gone.

"Nice touch, *asshole*. I hope you can hear me, cause *I'm not buying it*!"

Turning back to the computer, Tony read the decoded filenames, double clicking on a file entitled *Master Plan*.

LIB

"820 West Randolph."

The cabby pressed a button to start the meter and drove south on Michigan.

Her phone rang. *Tony*. She let it go to voicemail.

The cabby turned right on Lake.

She'd seen recent photos of Pat. He looked the same except for the receding hair line. She knew they'd chitchat for a bit, but she'd quickly get down to business, pumping him for information. She went through the questions in her head beforehand — part of her training.

She paid the fare along with a tip in front of the Little Goat Diner located in the old meat packing district of Chicago — an area converting to trendy residential and many great restaurants.

Pat waved half a block away on the other side of a crowd gathered outside the door. They walked toward each other.

She tiptoed to hug the tall man, still lean. She stepped back and smiled.

His eyes traveled the length of her body. "You look exactly the same," he said.

"You, too."

"Let's get our name on the list, or we'll be here all day."

"Right."

She followed him through the crowd to a small counter

where a woman took Pat's name and his cell phone number to text when a table became available.

"You like the *Trib*?"

"It's okay. It's a bit confining."

"Yeah, I thought you'd say that."

They wandered to the bar end of the restaurant, looking at merchandise for sale.

"How 'bout you? You like being the AG?"

"It's a headache sometimes.   Nothing like student government."

Lib recalled that Pat had been President. He caught the bug early, no doubt following up with a career in government service. He could do more, he'd said to her once.

"Pat, what's your take on these shootings?"

"I don't like it."

She smiled at him, her way of disarming interviewees.

"I mean, what needs to change, Pat?"

"You know me too well."

She smiled again. It wasn't to tease him, so much as an acknowledgement. Maybe she'd gain a few extra points.

He continued.   "I think we need major reform in our system of justice."

"I thought you'd say that."

"Why's this important to you?"

"I think you know."

Pat looked at his phone. "Our table's ready."

They walked back to the dining area then followed a waitress with two menus to their table.

Pat continued. "Yeah, I think I know what's driving this, but I want to hear you say it. I have a reason for asking."

"I'd like to do something to help. I want to make a difference."

"I think we can do something as a team."

BILL

Dickens' red Ferrari gleamed under the overhead lights in the reserved space. Bill admired the sleek lines, standing next to Cherise in the parking deck of Trump Tower. Unlocking the door, he struggled to insert himself into the cockpit, weaving his lanky frame under the steering wheel and onto the seat — only inches above the pavement. Cherise opened the passenger door and sat, drawing her long legs inside, tilting them against the center console, her knees pressed together.

Surrounded by instruments, Bill felt the compression of the capsule as they closed their doors. He adjusted the seat and inserted the key into the ignition, pressing the clutch and the brake, wiggling the shift into neutral, inhaling the leathery interior. In his mind, ground control counted down from ten before he turned the key, the engine roaring in response.

He slid the shift into reverse and slowly raised his foot on the clutch pedal, the tires barking on the pavement before killing the engine. Cherise giggled.

"Let the engine catch before giving it just a little gas," she offered.

Bill tried again, this time lurching rearward before depressing the clutch and brake simultaneously, the engine still running. He released the brake and gunned the engine with the clutch still engaged, enjoying the echo of the signature whiny roar, quickly rising and falling in pitch in response to his foot on the gas.

"Just let the car roll," Cherise advised. "Don't give it too much gas, it'll get away from you."

Crashing Mr. Dickens' Ferrari would not be a good way to start my first day on the job, Bill thought. He followed her instructions, easing down one level to a gate attendant who waved at Cherise. Rumbling under the raised gate, Bill drove out of the parking garage onto the street.

The sun reflecting on the polished hood of the car, they drove along Michigan Avenue amid the usual array of cars, busses and taxi cabs. On the sidewalks, shoppers mixed with street vendors and tourists — many turning their heads to watch them pass. Bill felt something new — occasionally revving the engine — treating the onlookers to the sound of Italian engineering and bravado. They turned on Lake Street and again into a public parking deck located a block from the Miracle Mile — not very far from the hotel, but a lot more fun than walking.

Cherise had led Bill from shop to shop, selecting a complete wardrobe of clothing, paying with the company credit card and arranging for the clothes to be delivered — all except a pair of Gucci pants and a Hugo Boss shirt which Bill wore along with his new Ferragamo shoes, a pair of Ray Ban sunglasses and a Rolex watch.

Though not his style, Bill didn't want to insult his boss or his personal assistant. Yet, somehow, walking outside with Cherise gave him a new perspective. He enjoyed the sights and sounds of the city, discovering a part of himself that he didn't know existed.

Cherise had drawn Bill's attention several times during the day. Her face was like a porcelain doll, complete with pouty red lips.

"Let's grab dinner," Cherise offered.

Bill looked at his new watch. Ten minutes after six. "Okay."

Cherise lifted her phone and said, "Sixteen." They walked back to the car while she held the phone to her ear, waiting for a response.

"Hi, this is Cherise. Six-thirty table for two, please." She hung up the phone and smiled at him as they approached the car.

They wound their way out of the parking deck, onto Lake Street then onto Michigan Avenue, heading back to Trump Tower. Threading through traffic on one of the busiest roads in the country, Bill tasted ambition perhaps for the first time in his life. He could adjust to it.

"If I had a car like this, I would never let anyone drive it in the city."

Cherise laughed. Something about the laugh gave Bill a sense of comfort, a feeling of new friendship.

LIB

Pat had kissed her on the cheek after hailing a cab for her. He'd closed the door and waved from the sidewalk.

Her thoughts remained on their conversation. She could write a general piece and pitch it to her editor as timely and relevant, hopefully moving public opinion in a different direction.

She felt the familiar tug of idealism, a dream of a better society. How could she frame it into a printable form to satisfy her editor while offering substance?

* * *

Tony's cubicle was empty, like most of the surrounding cubicles on a warm sunny afternoon. Thousands flocked outside, a rite of early Summer after enduring the snow and the wind. Everyone understood. Besides, they were all measured on content. The old days of clicking typewriters and shouting editors had given way to text messaging and telecommuting. She decided to work in the quietness of her cube. She could focus better without the distractions of so many people celebrating their release from captivity.

* * *

She ran up the stairs to Bill's apartment, wanting to feel the warmth of his skin — her solace — her base. Using the key he'd given her to his apartment, she opened the door, laying her iPad and purse on the counter. "Bill?"

Rex trotted up to her so she stooped down and scratched his ears, watching his nubby tail wag approval. She, like Bill, had become part of the dog's small world. "Bill?!" she called again. The clock said six forty-five. She'd lost track of time, but felt she'd accomplished something for the day.

She walked into the bedroom — smiling at the wrinkled sheets. Maybe Bill'd gotten the job on the spot. That would be nice, perhaps adding more puzzle pieces to the picture of contentment she held in her mind — a picture that included a man with a solid career. She still couldn't make out whether her part of the image included a briefcase or an apron. The image had a dog, but a noticeable void existed off to the side. She knew what it represented, but didn't want to fill it in. At least, not yet.

The mechanical doorbell on the front door clanked a dull bing boong sound, so she walked back and peered through the sight glass at Tony. "We're closed!" she teased before opening the door and inviting him in.

"Where's Bill?"

"He had a meeting at Trump Tower. I thought he'd be back by now."

"He's probably having a beer with the guys," Tony said.

Lib smiled at the intentional absurdity of Tony's suggestion. "I don't think Bill drinks beer."

"What?" Tony smiled. "How can you trust a guy who doesn't drink *beer*?!"

"Maybe he's having milk with the boys," Lib countered.

They both laughed. Lib visualized an image of Bill with a milk mustache.

"He seems like a really nice guy, Lib." He looked sincere.

"That's nice of you to say."

"Well, maybe I've been a jerk."

Lib studied his face, looking for a crack through which to pry her investigative instinct. "Do I *know* you?"

"Seriously. I don't wanna lose you as a friend."

Wow. What a difference a day makes, she thought. Tony leaned against the wall as Lib inspected the contents of the refrigerator, wondering what to do about dinner.

"I found something," Tony began, leaning against the cased door opening, "Bernie talks about the U.S. dollar in one of the files. It's clear he didn't fully understand, but he said something about a collapse."

"That's not good. Our dollar is the standard. If it collapses, it would take years to rebuild a system of trade around the world and we'd be reduced to a bartering system in the interim."

"Yeah. I did some research. Our debt levels are so high, a market crash scenario, if possible, could result in massive credit defaults, freezing almost all economic activity around the world."

"How could someone do that?" Lib felt his eyes on her as she bent over and inspected the cabinets.

"I'm not sure, but after reading into it, I think a cyber attack could be a problem."

"I don't get it."

"What if someone could hack into the mainframes that store all the contracts? I'm talking about the Forex and the Nasdaq computers in which options are traded."

"Options?"

"Yeah. A lot of folks don't realize the size of these so-called derivatives markets. I'm still trying to wrap my head around it, but apparently, these markets are huge. They're many times larger than world GDP."

"Seriously?"

"It's hard to imagine, but these markets are mostly unregulated. The crisis in 2008 was partly due to mortgage lending practices, but there was something far more dangerous."

"Um hm." Lib waited for him to continue, still poking around in the cabinets.

"The real trouble happened when credit default swaps, a contractual form of insurance against bundles of mortgage-backed securities, another derivative, froze the credit markets."

"Sounds complicated."

"You got that right. Anyway, when the valuations on mortgages were in question, suddenly, there was a problem with the insurance contracts against default."

"Remind me again, what does this have to do with Bernie?"

"What if someone could buy and sell phony contracts? What if someone could monkey with the data on which valuations are made?"

"Wait a minute." Lib stood up from her crouched position where she'd inspected Bill's cleaning supplies. "Are you suggesting that someone could collapse the world economy by hacking into a computer?"

"I'm wondering if it's possible. I also found out that derivative markets help us maintain liquidity, or cash flow, allowing for world markets to thrive like living organisms. If you take away the cash flow, everything stops. Period. Nothing."

"Wow. That opens a ton of issues."

"Yeah. I'm talking major conflict," Tony said.

Lib smiled. "You know what? I can't worry about the end of the world. I need to come up with something to make for dinner."

Tony chuckled. "Nice. We might be in a position to save the world, and you've launched into Betty Crocker mode."

Lib gave a faux smile, each index finger pressed into her dimples with her head tilted.

Tony said, "I can see you in a domestic role. Little Bills runnin' around."

"Was that a dig?"

"No. Why would that be a bad thing?"

She checked the pantry again. Cereal on three shelves.

Tony said, "If Bill gets a regular job, you can quit the Trib and become a domestic engineer."

"Now, that was a dig."

"Sorry."

"Actually," she thought aloud, "it's not that bad of an image." She wanted to try it on for size, just to see how it fit. *Would Bill make a good father? His heart was in the right place.*

BILL

"You have a good heart, I can tell," Cherise said.

"Thank you."

Their meal was not like anything Bill had before in his life. It was one of two options from a tasting menu and the food came out in small portions. They sat at a table near a large window overlooking the Tribune Tower. He wondered about Lib. Maybe he should have called her.

"Excuse me, I need to make a phone call."

Bill folded his napkin and placed it on the table next to his milk before standing and walking outside into an area visible from their table. He watched Cherise sip her wine, waiting for Lib to answer.

"*Hello?*"

"Hi Lib."

"*Where are you?*"

"I'm on the sixteenth floor of the Trump Tower, having dinner."

A pause. "*I was worried. You should have called.*"

"I am so excited. I have a new job at Dickens and Associates. You will not believe it. I drove a Ferrari today and I am wearing leather pants and a silk shirt."

"*Wait a minute . . . slow down.*"

"I have an office and a personal assistant. In fact, I am having dinner with her right now."

She didn't respond.

"Lib?"

"*I'm here.*"

"I thought I lost the signal. Cherise is so pretty, and she helped me pick out clothes today."

"*I see.*"

"You will really like her. And, you will really like my new boss, Mr. Dickens."

"*Oh?*"

"Yes, he is a very nice man and he has a lot of money."

"*What exactly is this new job?*"

"I don't know yet. I have a big office with a view of Lake Michigan."

"*Hmmmmm. What does Mr. Dickens do?*"

"He helps people who have no friends."

"*Augh! Bill, I'm not waiting up for you. Have a nice time.*"

"Okay."

The signal was gone.

Cherise looked at him from the table and waved. He waved back. It was so nice of Lib to understand.

Walking back into the restaurant, he noticed that Cherise had placed the company credit card into a black folder. She had done so much for him all day and he wanted to do something back. He wanted to pay for the meal. He lifted the black folder and looked at the check then put it back down with her credit card still tucked into the small pocket.

"Thank you so much for dinner," he said.

"You're welcome."

"I called my friend Lib. She told me to have a good time."

"That's nice." Cherise smiled at him. "Maybe we can go over to Roof."

"What roof?"

She laughed. "It's a rooftop lounge on the top of the Wit hotel, silly."

"That sounds like fun. Can we drive?"

She studied him through the corner of her eyes, a coy look on her face. "I don't think so. I think you've had a little too much to drink," pointing at Bill's near empty glass of milk. "Seriously, we should leave the Ferrari here and just walk two blocks to the Wit."

"Okay."

They walked under the streetlights amid tall buildings. People showed little fear in the main business districts, despite the recent events. Bill knew that other areas of town were not so fortunate. He felt safe.

Cherise played hopscotch, tip-toeing in her high-heeled shoes on the sidewalk. "Now you try it," she called, fifteen feet ahead of him.

Bill looked at the chalk squares and emulated Cherise's movements — *one leg, two legs, one leg, two legs*.

"Very good!" she said, wrapping her arms around him as he jumped from the final square. She looked up at him and then kissed him on the cheek, near the corner of his mouth, and then she pushed herself back, grabbed his hand and ran across the street with him in tow. "We're here," she said.

A line of people dressed in fancy clothes stood outside of the hotel on the sidewalk. A man at the door waved at Cherise, so they walked around the crowd, through the side door of the modern glass and metal building. An attendant motioned near the elevators and stepped inside the elevator long enough to use a key card, pressing twenty-seven before saying, "Have a good time." The doors closed. Cherise still held Bill's hand. She swung both their hands back and forth, humming a song that Bill didn't know.

Pulsating sounds summoned from above as the elevator

neared the top floor of the Wit hotel. The door opened and the sound got much louder. They walked past several large men in dark suits into a glassed in area with multi colored lights revolving, casting images on the people and the glass walls and the bar. A view of the Chicago skyline surrounded an eclectic mix of well-dressed young adults, some dancing, others laughing and trying to talk above the throbbing music.

"What are we doing here?!"   Bill shouted above the noise.

"I thought you didn't drink beer!" Cherise shouted back.

Bill moved close to Cherise's ear and repeated his question so she could hear him.   Her hair smelled like flowers.

She leaned over and spoke into his ear, her hand cupped over.   "We're having fun.   Remember what Lib told you." Her lips grazed his ear as she spoke.

TONY

Back in Lib's downstairs apartment, Tony continued reading through Bernie's files. *So much wasted potential.*

He sipped his coffee, sitting at the table borrowed from Bill's, trying to make sense of the folders and file names — there were so many. One folder caught his eye. Mayor. He could see from the thumbnails, they were all FLV files with timestamps. Tony double clicked one, launching a video player with controls overlaying a still image. He clicked the forward arrow and watched the back of a man's head shift into motion — then into full view, walking around a desk and speaking to someone. It was Mayor Jay Epstein, talking to his secretary over an intercom.

How did Bernie do it? How could he get a camera into the mayor's office?

Tony found another file folder called shower. Hundreds of thumbnails, each revealing girls showering in what appeared to be a dormitory. He watched a few of them — part of his research.

A funny noise startled him. A Facetime call. Lena. Tony exited the shower video playing on his screen and answered the call.

She wore makeup and seemed a bit more business-like, in a nice white blouse and lime green jacket. Her hair was pulled back revealing an oval face with high cheekbones. She sipped her coffee.

"*Good morning,*" she said.

"Morning."

"*What're you doing?*"

"Nothing much," Tony chortled, "just reading about a guy."

"*Hmmmmm.*"

"No! Not like *that*."

"*I'll bet.*" She smiled. So fresh and innocent looking.

"I'm a writer. I spend a lot of time doing research."

"*I know. I'm just kidding.*"

She took another sip. He'd wondered if she'd call back.

"*Just want to remind you again, you're not alone.*" She paused. "*Well . . . I guess maybe you are alone, but you don't have to be.*"

"Okay, here it comes."

She smiled again. "*I don't want your money. I'm not selling anything.*"

"Are we on the same planet?"

"*Excuse me?*"

"The world, as I know it, doesn't work that way."

She nodded in agreement. "*Yes, but, you can make a difference. We can make a difference.*"

"Okay. You've got my attention. Let's hear it."

She looked down at her desk and Tony could hear a scrawling ink pen — out of view of the camera. "*Okay, just a second.*" When she looked up, her face was a little less cheerful, perhaps a bit sad and compassionate — a look he'd often received from his counselor in high school.

"*Tony. I know you're struggling right now, but I hope you'll hear me out. Will you hang in there with me for a minute?*"

"Sure. Go."

Her eyebrows arched, a deliberate sign that something

important was about to happen. It was all the same with these folks. Tony prepared himself for the delivery. Maybe it was a new spin on selling timeshares.

"My job is to help people like you, Tony. I was in the same boat just two months ago until I discovered a network of people who've changed my life."

Tony sat back in the chair with his arms folded. He nodded with a half smirk.

"I've discovered that I can reach out to others and . . . "

He cut her off. "Are you with a time share?"

"No. Absolutely not. We offer support to each other."

"We?"

"Thousands of people are struggling just like you and me. Rejection. Despair. Something had to change."

"Moonies?"

"Nope. We provide a home base for those who've been squeezed out. Some folks move on with a renewed vigor. We wish them well and let them follow their own paths. Others, like myself, decide to stay. We want to give something back."
Lena bit her lower lip, her eyes showing interest.

"What's in this for me?"

"Acceptance. You become part of a network of folks."

"How much does it cost?"

"I already told you. I'm not selling anything. I'm here for you, just like someone was here for me."

Tony played along, rubbing his chin with his thumb and index finger. "Okay, so what now? What's the next step?"

"We buy you dinner. You come to our offices and we introduce you to a group of folks who'll share their experience with you."

"This really freaks me out just a little. I don't even know you."

Lena looked like a child whose balloon had floated away

and then her eyes darted past him. "*Oh. I didn't realize you have someone with you.*"

Tony spun around. "Dude!" He heard Lena say goodbye. "Why are you *doing* this to me?"

"She's not for you, cupcake."

"How do you know that? I'll be the judge of who I talk to online."

"Just watch yourself, sonny. Things are not always as they seem."

"But . . .,"

Michael cut him off. "I'd love to chat with you all day, but I need you to do something."

"What? Are you serious?"

"How can I not be serious? Look at me."

Tony looked at him. *He had a point. He did look serious.*

Michael continued. "You need to talk to your friend, Lib. Not the usual drivel — really talk to her."

Tony winced at the dig, but wasn't in the mood to drill into Michael's communications style. "What about?"

"Have you read her editorial piece in the paper?"

"Not yet."

"I suggest you read it."

"Okay, you still haven't told me what to talk about. What do I say?"

"Don't ask me. Ask him." MIchael lifted his eyes to the ceiling for a fraction of a second, then looked back at Tony. "He'll give you the right words."

"Bill?"

"No, you goofball. God."

They stood a moment in silence, Tony trying to absorb it. "If this is so important, why don't you get involved?"

"Good question, cupcake. I can't. I can only work

through others . . . like you."

Tony grabbed the Tribune, searching for the article.

THE DRUG/GUN CONNECTION
By Lib Rand

If you take a minute to Google "drug related gun violence," it may surprise you. I received 30 million hits. A percentage of the articles posit a growing sentiment among ordinary, law abiding citizens that the drug war is causing much more harm than good.

To be clear, I'm not an advocate for drug use. However, it seems that any fair discussion or debate about gun control would address the connection that exists between illegal drugs and gun violence. It's not a comfortable position for anyone, but the argument is compelling. In short, a black market for drugs is thriving in America today. Drug dealers are armed and they're dangerous.

Nobody wants to see kids hooked on drugs. At the same time, nobody wants to see kids gunned down in the street. But, after 40 years, we have the highest incarceration rate in the world and the problem is worse than ever while the underlying black market for drugs is more organized. I live in the Chicago area, so I recently looked at local statistics related to organized crime.

Though Chicago's population is three times smaller than New York City, the murder rate is nearly four times higher according to ABC News. Chicago has 100,000 gang members with only 12,000 police officers. In 2011, 61% of all homicides were gang related with 59 known gangs in Chicago.

By the way, Chicago has strict gun control laws. On a national level, it's likely that gun control laws will create yet another black market and it will have no more impact on gun violence than drug laws have on drug use. In reality, our drug laws are creating opportunities for criminals and it's obvious that authorities have no control over the gangs and the drug cartels.

Please, don't take my word for it. Google it for yourself. I would encourage anyone to look at the statistics. Look at the vast majority of gun related deaths, where they occur and how it impacts large segments of our population.

Frankly, I believe it's our unwillingness to look at the problem objectively. Today's polarized political environment is more about condemnation and demagoguery and less about working together to solve a serious national issue. No matter how strongly we feel about the moral aspects, it pays to look at this problem closely.

The system of illegal drug distribution (gangs and cartels) is more of a problem than the drugs themselves. We don't know who they are and where they live and how they integrate into our communities. Black markets don't have a national registry. Drug lords don't care who gets the drugs and who they have to kill to hold onto their power base.

Many narcotics are legal in this country. An overwhelming majority of narcotics listed in the Physician's Desk Reference are distributed by hospitals, doctors and pharmacies. Meanwhile, a black market distribution system is empowered by a handful of drugs classified as Schedule I. This same distribution system also gains access to large quantities of Schedule II drugs. It's the distribution system far more than the Schedule I drugs killing our kids.

It's ironic that our failed attempts to control drugs is now at the heart of gun violence in this country. It's also ironic that some folks want to continue in the same direction that empowered the black market for drugs — the very same mistake, I believe, that led to gun violence during alcohol prohibition.

The answer? I don't know with certainty. However, it's time to look at it objectively without politicizing the issue. Sadly, it's no longer possible to talk openly about sensitive topics. How can we solve a problem if we cannot talk about it?

LIB

The phone rang. It was Tony's ring. *Not now*. He had the worst timing of any human being on earth. *Just let it go to phone mail*, she thought.

Thirty seconds later, it rang again. *What's up with you*?! "Hello!!"

"Lib, I need to talk to you."

"Now?"

"Yeah, but I'd rather talk to you in person."

"*Jeez* Tony. I'm not *dressed*."

"I'll give you ten minutes."

"Tony, I . . ." She looked at her phone. The connection was lost.

"*Augh*!" She picked up a few items then marched to the bathroom and turned on the shower. He would have to wait.

She undressed — gathering her things and laying them on the countertop before stepping into the shower. She wouldn't take the time to enjoy the hot water running through her hair and down her body. Instead, she launched into late mode, quickly soaping herself — washing and rinsing her hair.

What's up with him? she thought. *Maybe letting him move in downstairs was a mistake.*

She quickly dried herself and then wrapped an oversized towel around her body before drying her hair with another smaller towel.

The doorbell rang. "Just a *minute!*" she called. It rang again followed by pounding on the door.

She walked to the front door, peeked to make sure and then opened it before turning back toward the bedroom. Hearing him close the door, she knew he watched her.

Not today pervert, she thought, closing the bedroom door, blocking his view. She jumped into Bill's gym shorts and a tee shirt before returning, finding him sitting on the couch in the living room, petting Rex.

"Okay. So what could possibly be so important?"

"First of all, six folks were gunned down at Union Station last night."

"Good boy, Rex." He rubbed the dog's ears.

"That's *it*?"

"Six people *died*, Lib. They haven't caught the shooter."

"What's going *on* with you, Tony?"

He continued to scratch Rex. "Whaddya mean?"

"It just so unusual to hear you take such an interest in this way."

"I care. Maybe I don't always *talk* about it like *you*, but I care."

"What happened to Mr.-All-About-Tony? What happened to the opportunist?"

Tony looked down at the dog. "I don't know. I've been thinking a lot lately."

"What's this about, Tony?"

His eyes looked tired. He returned his attention to her.

"I was so proud to get through school." He ran his finger along the piping on the edge of the seat cushion, first along the front — then following its curvature around the side. "I had this great vision. I wanted to spend a few years, paying my dues, then write the great American novel."

"You never told me that before."

"Yeah, it's kinda like a jinx to talk about something that you can't get off the ground. I don't talk about it much with anyone really."

She waited. He had something to say. *One Mississippi, two Mississippi . . .*

"I love the classics.   Guys like Hemmingway and Fitzgerald and Harper Lee."

"Harper Lee's a woman."

"Really?"

Lib gently shook her head — wanting to say something — but kept it to herself.

"Anyway, I love a good story.   These days, the competition is crazy. Readers have short attention spans, so writers must sacrifice their principles to break through."

"Principles? Who *are* you?

"I have principles."

"Okay, okay. . . ,"

He was serious — his tired eyes now expressing pain. *One Mississippi, two Mississippi . . .*

"Even the news, Lib."

He rarely called her by name. *Strange.*

"It's become a form of entertainment.   They're pandering to their audience. I don't think they really care anymore."

"Hey, give it time to run it's course. Folks will get tired of the media hoopla and demand substance."

"I'm not so sure. Folks want blood and guts. They want the seedy side of humanity."

"C'mon Tony. You're starting to worry me."

"It's extremism, Lib.   Everything's over the top. Otherwise, nobody cares anymore."

"I think you're stereotyping."

"Look around. It's in the news. It's on television. It's

in the movies. It's in books. Now, ordinary people are following the same pattern. We have folks raging about overreaching government on one end and people on the other end raging about excess wealth and the dangers of a free market society. We were just talking about it. What happened to balance? Where does it go from here?"

"Have you been watching Joel Osteen?"

He cut his eyes at her — a flash of passion. Maybe he needed a little push. "That's it, isn't it?" she continued. "You're getting religion."

"Lib. We have a responsibility. I've never regretted anything that I've written. Believe me, I've given thought to it. I wondered if I could have a better life if I followed the trend. I can't do it. It's not who I am."

"Is this about my article?"

"Just *think* about it Lib. You can't take it *back*."

"I don't *want* to take it back."

"Lib, you're responding to an extreme with an extreme."

Lib shook her head from side to side. "The liberals and conservatives are the extremists. I want balance."

"I think I know where you're coming from. Yes, our incarceration rates are off the charts. The courts are backed up. We've diluted the justice system while empowering organized crime."

"Yes," she said.

"It's like Prohibition in the 1920's."

"So."

"But you can't just fling open the door and say, 'Get your meth and crack here.'"

"I'm not advocating open distribution without control. I'm advocating controls on dangerous substances."

"You'll never convince the American people. Besides, I thought we were working together to find Jack."

"We *are*. It's just a piece on gun violence, *that's* all."

Tony looked around as though he just remembered something. "Where's Bill?"

She sighed. "He didn't come home last night."

"Well, there it is again. Computer geek stays out all night. I'm telling you, these are strange times we're in."

LIB

Tony's comments gnawed at her — driving her jeep on I-88 through the western suburbs. When she needed a break from the city, she sought rural scenes to help her unwind. The cornfields and the silos and the barns might help her through a bout with her conscience.

Still in traffic, Lib thought about Tony's response to her article. Somehow, she'd added to his pain, perhaps unintentionally betraying his trust. Why didn't he understand her need to speak her mind?

Maybe Tony expected her to follow his lead. In truth, she didn't share the same level of interest in Michael and his conspiracy theories. The old man had spooked Tony with all the end-of-the-world stuff. Besides, no matter how compelling the story, the words of an old man and a few file references on a dead man's computer weren't enough. Tracking someone with an alias had even less potential for paying off. She simply followed her own instinct, submitting her article without consulting Tony.

His reaction had surprised her. He'd rarely said anything, but she knew he'd admired her work in the past. His admiration and respect were quiet. It's how she knew. Others gushed over her articles. Not Tony. He'd find some detail — some omission or perhaps a point on style on which to critique her work. Never once did he go toe-to-toe on the issues. It was always about the writing. Tony, the mentor, had offered his experience. This time, she'd gone around him, sweet-talking the editor. *Was it his pride, or was it a moral issue for him?*

She'd embraced her self-reliance. She was smart. She was pretty. She was practical and resourceful. She knew how to get things done. Her belief in herself was an asset. Her selfishness was human nature and she'd found it easier to dismiss the guilt that would only slow her down. How could she stop and consider every possible angle? It was better to just accept it and move on.

Yet, she felt uncomfortable with the thought of her father in the dream accepting her brief foray into drugs. He would've never accepted it, just as he'd never accepted her Libertarian position after she'd moved to Cambridge.

By her sophomore year, her worldview had been clear, but it was fuzzy again. Tony had caught her off guard with the comment about meth and crack. She'd seen the billboards of kids with rotten teeth, resembling zombies. How do you explain the concept of free will to a mother who's lost a child to meth or crack or heroin? She'd responded to the issue of gangs without regard for those who depend on protection through a healthy system of justice.

Somewhere in the fuzzy picture, an elusive common thread had to bind it all together. Somewhere, a single answer must exist for a world gone completely mad. *What was it?* Some people are climbing over one another to get ahead while others are responding with violence. *What are they responding to? Where's the imbalance?*

Only a short time back, she'd felt confident that the balance was naturally occurring. Freedom was the answer to all of her questions — that is, until one man's freedom became another man's nightmare. Until *her* freedom became another man's nightmare. Her neatly packaged belief system had given her comfort, but recent events caused her to question a self-regulating environment.

Bernie had responded. He'd cracked under pressure from his environment, perhaps from something within. Either way, it was a response. An extreme response. *Was he bullied?* In turn, she'd responded to him. It was a clash of extreme behaviors, resulting in his death and a cover-up. What about the mayor? He'd responded with authority and control — an attempt to restore order by way of yet another extreme. Maybe she'd reacted to the ban on guns — the potential loss of liberty once guaranteed by the Constitution.

Going after guns without first addressing the root cause for violence and extreme behaviors made no sense to her. She wished she'd pointed it out to Tony. They were simply looking at extremism from two different angles, both agreeing on the impact, but failing to recognize their common ground.

Lib passed an old exit — once the gateway to prosperity for a few small business owners. An empty shopping plaza stood in the center of a long neglected parking lot — surrendering itself to nature — tall grass growing through cracks.

In her mind, Libertarianism had been the answer to prosperity. Businesses must have latitude. It's where jobs come from. America was built on industry and ingenuity, so why create an increasingly hostile business landscape with overregulation? That was her mantra for so long. Now it wasn't so clear.

Prosperity usually follows efficiency. It's the idea that the markets reward hard work and innovation. Yet, somehow, we've lost our way. The new environment has become thievish and corrupt — companies leveraging, absorbing and sometimes destroying the competition through economies of scale. Large companies can afford a massive infrastructure of accountants and lawyers and marketing professionals.

It was easier to accept her long-standing position without considering how conglomerates and mergers have the potential to destroy small businesses in this country. Eventually, in the game of Monopoly, there is but one winner who takes it all. Companies find ways to circumnavigate antitrust laws while the cost of doing business filters out the little guys. Markets do not feel. Markets do not see injustice. It's an extreme.

Brake lights and smoke in the distance caught her attention. She slowed and moved along at five miles per hour. A car lay upside down in the culvert, flames shooting through windows, several cars pulling over to assist. Traffic resumed speed twenty yards beyond the scene.

It wasn't like her at all. She didn't have regrets, much less about anything she'd written before. What was it? What else bugged her? Was it Tony?

Tony had a point. Things had gotten out of hand. Everything was extreme. Her tendency toward Libertarianism was a response to what she felt was an overreaching government. It was a response to a gnawing concern, perhaps even a fear of tyranny and a police state exemplified by a burgeoning prison system. Like our resistance to someone who pushes against us, we remain true to the dynamics of human behavior, pushing back. Individuals and groups react to their environment until they become the problem.

She wanted kids, though she'd already hit snooze on the mommy clock a few times. Survival of the fittest wasn't the ideal environment for raising a child. She wanted equal opportunity for them. She wanted her children to find careers in a healthy business environment. Something was missing.

Meanwhile, guys like Bill deserved a place in society. He had a lot to contribute, yet he was vulnerable to abuse and neglect in a highly competitive environment. Shouldn't the market accept Bill for his value rather than his odd exterior? What happens to the meek when we're consumed by our ambition to get ahead at all costs?

She thought about Bill's comments to her on the phone. He'd driven a Ferrari. He was wearing fancy clothes and having dinner at a nice restaurant with his new personal assistant — a woman. A nice office working for a guy who helps people? It was just too good to be true. Something's wrong.

A man in a soiled three piece suit stood on the shoulder holding a sign. *"Dead End."*

She looked for the next exit.

TONY

Water shot high into the air at Buckingham Fountain, cascading down ornate tiers, Lake Michigan glistening in the distance.

"It was weird. I started talking about my career," Tony said.

"You think too much."

"Maybe I don't think enough. I could have come up with something better than that."

Michael fished a coin out of his pocket. He closed his eyes and tossed it into the fountain.

"What's that for?"

"Just a prayer."

Tony rolled his eyes. "Are other angels like you?"

"Not so much. I'm more of a specialist."

"Meaning?"

"I get the tough assignments."

PAP! PAP! PAP! Tony spun — a man 50 yards away fell on the grass. A nun ran toward the man writhing on the ground. She pulled a pistol out of her habit. *PAP!* The man's body jerked, then laid motionless. She put the gun back into her sleeve, looked at Tony, then walked in the opposite direction across Lakeshore Drive into a seemingly oblivious crowd of people.

"Anyway, I didn't really want this assignment," Michael continued, "but nobody else would take it, so . . ."

Tony interrupted him. "Did you *see* that?"

"Yeah, I saw it. So I tell 'em, he's not gonna listen to me. He's hard headed and full of himself. Nope. Gotta go down and try to straighten things out a bit."

Tony watched for the nun with a five o'clock shadow as they walked North along the sidewalk among in-line skaters and rickshaw style bicycles carrying tourists. Michael seemed to admire the sailboats. Despite his appearance, the man possessed an intriguing spiritual quality — an authority. Ordinarily, Tony would have called his editor. He would have called the police. Oddly, a man shot in broad daylight seemed of little consequence in relation to recent events and the threat of economic collapse.

"What's gonna happen to me, Michael?"

"You gotta stop worryin'. It doesn't do any good at all. Besides, like I told ya, you can't live up to your potential if you're consumed by fear."

"C'mon! It's *scary* down here, man!"

"Yeah, but look around," Michael said. "Fear drives people to extremes. The more fear, the more extremes. The more extremes, the more fear. It's a cycle."

"Maybe you're right. Maybe history's a good example."

"You're startin' to get it, cupcake. Yep, ol' history shows us over and over again. Do we learn from our mistakes? Nope. Right back where we started from. Then, we rebuild and do it all over again."

They walked fifty yards without speaking, a siren wailing in the distance.

The old man shaded his eyes, looking up at a hovering seagull screeching at them, begging for food.

"I'm not sure what to do," Tony said, kicking a cigarette butt.

"You gotta have faith. You gotta trust God."

"Yeah, like that *guy* back there. Look where it got 'im."

"Don't be fooled by everything you see."

Tony looked at his emotionless face. "You're not helping."

"So, why not give God a try? Just ask and see what happens."

Tony sighed. "If you're not here for me, then who're you here for?"

"Now, take somebody like Lib. She's got the potential to turn this mess around, if she can just get her head screwed on right."

"I got news for ya, she thinks she's some kinda great humanitarian, but she's no different than everybody else. She's selfish. She just plays a better game, convincing others of her compassion."

"Some of us start out that way, cupcake. Give 'er time."

"All this talk about sacrifice. I'm not sure I like this screenplay. Michael?"

Tony looked to both sides and behind him. He was gone.

"I've got to find Lib," he muttered, walking across Lakeshore, watching for the nun, heading southwest toward the Tribune tower.

Strange as it seemed, Michael offered compelling reasons to believe, though he didn't fit the Hollywood stereotype for a guardian angel.

Dear God, I don't know what to say, Tony prayed as he walked. *I'm not very good at this praying stuff, but I don't know what to do. Maybe I think too much. Maybe I try to fix it myself. I don't know. Please, help me find my way. Just give me a sign. Amen.*

The gothic revival lobby of the Tribune Tower, usually teeming with employees and tourists, seemed quiet, only a few folks passing through and a security guard standing with his hands folded in front of him. Making his way to the elevator, Tony heard a man talking about the U.S. dollar on a large screen television mounted to the wall.

"*We need to remain calm, Tony,*" the man said with a French accent on CNBC, winking at the camera. Tony read the name displayed below the man's image. Gerard leBanquier. "*The dollar remains the standard on which all currencies are measured,*" he continued.

The image went to a three way split screen, showing Mr. leBanquier, an analyst named Joseph Lamar from Goldman Sachs and the host of the program, Ron Albright. "*So, why is Goldman urging investors to buy gold?*" the host asked Mr. Lamar.

"*We feel the national debt issue hasn't been addressed. Gold is the best place to park at least a portion of a portfolio in case of a collapse. Look it up Wochowski.*"

Tony tilted his head and arched his eyebrows at the sound of his name spoken on the television.

Gerard leBanquier held up a finger, wanting to speak. "*Go ahead Mr. leBanquier,*" the host said.

"*It's all good,*" Mr. leBanquier said. "*History shows the U.S. Dollar is the most stable currency.*"

The elevator door opened and Tony stepped in, the man's words replaying in his mind. He'd heard it recently. *It's all good.* Bernie used the phrase many times.

Exiting the elevator at his floor, Tony walked past Lib's cubicle. Two people worked at their desks nearby, but the office was otherwise empty. Tony entered his cubicle and sat at his computer, ignoring his inbox.

He Googled Gerard leBanquier and began reading articles in which the man's name appeared. Mr. leBanquier had worked as Chief Information Officer at the Chicago Board of Trade. He was born in Calais, France, immigrating to the U.S. in the 70's. Tony clicked another link. Gerard recently served as advisor to a task force, helping to design cyber security for online trading.

His heart pounding, he continued reading.

Gerard accepted an executive position at Dickens and Associates. He helped grow the private assets of the firm to $32 billion, hedging securities investments with options strategies.

Tony scanned the other links, looking for something recent. One article had been posted ten minutes earlier. Tony clicked it.

DICKENS AND ASSOCIATES DUMPING SECURITIES, SHORTING DOLLAR, ASSOCIATED PRESS. The article contradicted Gerard's comments on CNBC. *Why would Dickens and Associates shift positions while calling for calm?* Maybe Michael was right. Maybe an attack was eminent. Maybe Gerard was establishing a position to benefit from market volatility, but how would he know? If anyone knew how to time the markets, they'd soon own everything in the world. What if Gerard knew how to impact the market? What if he found a way through the same firewalls he helped to design?

Tony Googled options trading, reading a few of the links on the first page. He found a recent link from *Investor's Business Daily.* Contracts were at all time highs. What if Gerard found a way into the system? He could easily crash the markets!

BILL

The thin sliver of light in the dark room seemed unusual. He tried to remember. *Oh yes. It was late.* He was at the Wit hotel. He stood and pulled the heavy curtains apart.

"Good morning."

He turned around. Cherise smiled at him from the other side of the king-sized bed. He looked down at himself. Fully dressed. The covers slid back on the bed. Cherise slipped out and stepped naked into the bathroom.

This is not a good way to begin a business relationship, he thought to himself as he peeked out at The Renaissance Hotel across the street. He would explain it all to Lib. She would understand.

Cherise came back out with a towel wrapped around her. "I'd like to take a shower. I'll meet you at the office." She closed the door.

Bill walked through an opening into the other side of the contemporary suite. He'd had a glass of wine at the bar, but he didn't remember going to the room with Cherise. She'd arranged for the room after they left Roof really late. He'd said goodbye to her at the desk. She'd kissed him on the lips and waved as he turned back toward the elevator.

Bill grabbed a croissant out of a basket on the way to the door, pausing before walking into the hallway. Cherise sang in the shower.

It was too much sensory information for him. He'd

lived a semi-ordinary life until Lib arrived. Now, he'd perhaps broken out of his shell into something very different. Yet, something didn't feel right. He changed his mind about telling Lib. She would not understand. He didn't understand.

An ominous cloud approached from the west. Bill, still wearing the Gucci pants and Hugo Boss shirt, walked a few blocks north on Wabash to Trump Tower.

Droplets of rain began to fall as he ducked under the portico, making his way to the elevator. A man walked with Bill and keyed the elevator, allowing him access to the offices of Dickens and Associates.

The Rolex watch felt huge on his arm, embarrassing him. Painfully aware of his uncharacteristic attire, he wanted his Dockers and a flannel shirt.

Wanda sat at her desk. The smile from the day before had faded.

"Good morning," Bill said.

"Mornin'." She did not look up.

Bill walked straight across to his office, looking outside at the surrounding clouds. He couldn't see the street or Lake Michigan.

He sat and turned on the computer, selecting CNN.com. Someone would direct him eventually, so, he sat reading the headlines.

A link entitled "The Drug/Gun Connection" caught his attention — an article from the *Chicago Tribune* written by Lib Rand.

"I see you've returned. I'll take that as a yes response to my offer."

Bill saw Mr. Dickens's reflection in the adjacent monitor.

"Good morning sir," Bill said, turning around in his

chair and standing to shake his boss's hand.

Dickens' skin felt cold.   He looked past Bill at his computer.

"Interesting article."

"Yes, I was just reading it."

"Seems Ms. Rand is of the Libertarian persuasion."

"I guess so."

"I like her."

Dickens looked out at the clouds.

"I like her too," Bill said.

"You don't have to like people or things just because I do."

"No, I mean I really like her. Actually, I love her."

Dickens turned and raised his eyebrows.

"She's my girlfriend. Well, at least I think she's my girlfriend. She's living at my apartment . . . I uh . . . , we've slept together."

"That certainly qualifies, son. Congratulations!"

"For what, sir?"

"For scoring the big one. Landing the big fish."

"Oh."

Dickens sat in a chair opposite Bill's desk.

"So, how do you like your office?"

"It's very nice."

"How about your personal assistant?"

He looked over his reading glasses.

"She's very nice too."

"I can get you another one if you'd prefer."

"Oh no. I mean. We've only just met."

"Okay. If you change your mind, just let me know."

"Okay."

Dickens rested his elbows on the arms of the chair, his fingers together at the tips, resembling a pyramid. "Did you catch the financial news?"

"Uh, no sir."

"Dow's down hard this morning. A lot of big companies are missing their estimates."

The comment seemed out of place. Maybe his new job would soon come to an end if the markets crashed. "What does this mean for you?"

"Don't take this the wrong way, son. You'll find out soon enough. It's all good for Dickens and Associates."

"I see." Bill usually didn't pay much attention to the stock market. He understood it well enough, it just did not appeal to him.

Dickens stood and stepped back toward the window. The clouds hung thick around the building like a dark gray quilt. Bill stood up and looked out at the clouds — shoulder to shoulder with Mr. Dickens, who stood, hands in his pockets. Bill put his hands into his pockets. A strange image flashed in front of them, an earthbound figure in the clouds accelerating downward at thirty-two feet per second squared before disappearing into the thick gloom. It looked like a man. Actually, it looked a lot like a smiling Donald Trump, his cantilevered hair firmly in place.

"Yes, it's all good for Dickens and Associates."

LIB

Dickens was the man's name. His office was at Trump Tower. She'd find out for herself.

She felt around for it in the closet. *It has to be here somewhere.* Bill had returned it to the closet after leaving Bernie's. She felt something soft. It was the cloak. Finding the microswitch, she flipped it off, watching the cloak appear as the power used to project images onto the substrate dissipated.

Lib stood up in front of the mirror on the back of the closet door. She wrapped the cloak around herself, flipping the switch back on, peering through the slit as the shimmering image of the cloak wrapped around her body slowly began to display the image directly behind her.

Lib fed Rex before gathering her purse and the cloak, locking the door and making her way downstairs. She used the cloak to shield her from the rain that had begun to fall, running to her car, tossing her purse into the passenger seat, oblivious to the old Camaro sitting on the opposite side of the lot.

TONY

He waited for her to answer her phone. Voicemail. *Where could she be*? The rain came down harder, dripping through one of the holes down the back of his neck. Annoyed, he waited in the car for the rain to let up.

With new information, Lib might help put the pieces together. Somehow, Bill was the key. Tony wanted to demonstrate his value to Lib. He wanted to make a difference, but he had to set things right with her at the same time, feeling remorse for attacking her beliefs and her article.

Tony wiped the fog from inside the window, straining to see. Something moved. A pair of jeans ran across the parking lot holding a purse. Tony wiped the window again, then rubbed his eyes. The door to her Jeep opened, the jeans got into the car, then the door closed. He started his car, turning the defroster on high, waiting for the windshield to clear. Her car began to move without a driver. Tony eased out of the parking space and followed.

LIB

She lifted the wet cloak and placed it beside her, over her purse. Maybe the water had damaged it. She glanced at her purse laying on the seat beside her. Seems okay.

Traffic was heavy on Clark heading south. She went through the plan in her mind, thinking about Bill and his strange message. *Is he in danger? Is he with the woman? Jeez! Give a guy a little nookie and he turns into a hound!*

TONY

Following the driverless car, Tony watched Lib appear out of nowhere, sitting in the driver's seat. He leaned forward, pinching the bridge of his nose, hanging far enough back to escape notice.

Lib made her way down Clark. *Where's she going?*

Lib turned on Ohio then right on Wabash. Tony watched as she u-turned and pulled up to the valet stand at Trump Tower. She got out, carrying something under her arm. Turning his car around, he pulled in behind her Jeep as she stood outside the lobby of the hotel. Tony left the keys in the ignition and the door open for the valet — trotting to catch up to Lib, who'd vanished.

She'd said that Bill's new job was at Trump Tower. *What was the company? When did she say it?*

Something wasn't adding up. Stepping through the revolving door, Tony looked around. He'd lost her. *Shit*! Tony considered his options, pacing around the lobby, stopping momentarily to look at the directory in hopes that it might trigger his memory.

A nice looking strawberry blonde walked through the revolving door. *Where did he know her?*

She smiled. "Holy *cow*! What are *you* doing here?" Lena asked.

"I'm here to meet a friend."

"Oh, *really*?"

"Yeah, um . . . but, I don't know where she is right now."

"What's her name?"

"Lib Rand."

Lena tilted her head. "The reporter?"

"Yes."

"Maybe I can help you find her," Lena said, pushing a strand of hair around her ear. "Come with me."

Tony followed her across the lobby to the executive elevator. She was taller than he'd imagined. Nice butt.

A seated attendant — an overweight Afro American man — waved at her as she boarded the elevator.

"Sir, you can't go in there." He motioned for Tony to come out.

"It's okay, he's with me Charlie."

"Sorry."

The doors closed. She smiled at him again. "What a nice surprise meeting you here."

Tony smiled back. Maybe his luck had changed. Maybe he'd ask her out . . . later. *No. Now! Do it now! It's the end of the world, what can I lose?*

"Can I buy you coffee sometime?"

She giggled. "Sure. It's not like we're total strangers now, is it?"

He caught her eye. *Pretty. Maybe a little naughty too.*

"How 'bout dinner then?"

"That's even better." She tilted her head up with inviting eyes.

He leaned over and kissed her.

LIB

Looking around, Lib wrapped the cloak around herself, hoping nobody saw her behind a potted shrub, a few feet away from the main entry. Though difficult to walk at first, a few adjustments allowed her to shuffle through the revolving door and into the lobby.

Slowly, she made her away along the edge of the lobby, trying to avoid a collision. She waited at the executive elevators.

A minute later, Tony entered the building through the revolving doors. *What's he doing here?* He disappeared from her view for a moment, and then returned, standing in the middle of the lobby like a lost puppy dog. *What a goob.* He waved at somebody. *A girl. Tony has a girlfriend?*

Tony and the girl stood together in the lobby for a moment, talking. They approached her, stopping on the other side of the attendant from where she stood, waiting on the elevator to arrive. The doors opened. Lib edged behind the attendant, narrowly dodging the doors as they closed behind her.

They seemed to know each other. She watched and listened to the exchange, silently cheering for Tony as he leaned over and kissed her.

TOM AND GEORGE

Glued to the screen on the console, Tom and George watched Tony kiss Lena.

"Hit the stop button, fool!" Tom advised.

George cut his eyes at his friend. "Anybody ever tell you you're a dirty ol' man?"

Tom grinned, maintaining his vigil. "Yeah, I don't get out much."

"You don't get out at all."

Tom watched as the two exited the elevator. "Shoot!"

"I'm tellin' your wife."

"Go ahead. She's probably over at the pool, watchin' the lifeguard."

"Okay, so I'm tellin' your girlfriend."

Tom grimaced. "You're not right in the head. Sally's just a friend."

"Umm hmmm."

"Look at me," Tom swiveled toward his friend, his arms outstretched. "My mojo stopped workin' a long time ago."

"Yeah, but those old eyes . . ."

"I have a job to do, and so do you. Sometimes you see things."

"You're easily distracted. Everything we've worked for is at stake and you're looking for a cheap thrill. I'm callin' Michael."

LIB

The door opened and she followed them through the wood wall past the receptionist, and then through double glass doors into an open office area. Tony followed the girl to her cubicle.

Through the glass wall of a nice office ahead of her, Lib saw Bill sitting at his computer. She moved closer, stopping outside Bill's door, waiting and watching. *Someone will open the door.*

BILL

He sat wondering about the image he'd seen. A man falling from the top of a building typically required a response. *Was it real? Why didn't Mr. Dickens say something? Did he see it?* He'd simply dismissed himself and walked out of Bill's office, never saying a word about poor Mr. Trump.

Cherise walked toward the glass doors of his office from the lobby area. She entered and smiled, putting her purse down on a chair, then walked behind him, caressing his shoulders.

"Sleep well last night?"

"I think so."

She giggled.

"You were fan*tas*tic!"

"I was?"

She leaned over, hands still on his shoulders and kissed his cheek. "It's gonna be so much fun working here together."

"I . . . okay . . . I think so too."

He continued to read the news on his computer screen, though uncomfortable with her invasion of his space.

"Get used to your new office. I'm going to the little girl's room." Cherise announced, walking back out.

LIB

She'd deal with Bill later. Resisting the urge to reach out and strangle Cherise's Scandinavian neck, Lib quietly followed her back out among the cubicles, and then down a short corridor to the ladies' room.

Cherise stepped up to the mirror and touched up her lipstick as Lib stood in the corner watching, thinking of a dozen comments she might offer the bitch. Smiling at her wickedness, Lib thought it might be fun to say something really creepy and watch blondie jump out of her skin. *You know you just can't cover up slut with make-up, Cherise*, Lib thought. *How would that sound coming from a wall in the bathroom?*

Before Lib could speak, the door opened and a brown-haired woman walked in, stopping in front of the mirror beside Cherise, inspecting her makeup. "How's the new guy?"

"Oh, Bill?" Cherise laughed. "He's hooked."

Lib bit her lip. Something wasn't right.

Lib followed Cherise back out of the ladies' room. Blondie stopped to chat with someone at a cubicle, so Lib made a wide circle around, stopping at Bill's office, watching him through the glass, waiting for someone else to open the door for her. She couldn't risk Bill seeing or hearing the door open by itself. *One Mississippi, two Mississippi, three Mississippi, four . . . ,*

An older man wearing a dark suit emerged from a corner office at the other end of the room. "Mr. Dickens," Cherise said, walking past Lib, down the aisle between cubicles.

Cherise pointed back at Bill's office. The man nodded and began walking toward Lib. He hesitated for a second, looking in her direction before continuing. Maybe he thought of something. He completed his path to Bill's door, stopping just in front of her, pausing, opening the door and walking in. She followed.

"Bill. I'd like to meet that lovely girlfriend of yours. What's her name again?"

"Lib."

"Yes, Lib."

He paused for a second. "She seems like an amazing woman."

"Yes, I think so."

"Well, let's choose a good time to have dinner together. Maybe we can find a nice office for her as well."

Dickens patted Bill on the back before walking out. Lib stood between two ficus trees against the opposite interior wall, out of the main path in which she felt more likely to bump into someone.

It was strange to her. *How could Bill fall into such a situation? These things don't happen for guys like him.* He could make a decent living, sure, but Lib couldn't see him protecting his position among the ambitious elite. They'd entrap him or find a way to expose his weaknesses.

Like a mother watching a child's first day at school, she wondered how hard it must be as a parent to stand at a distance, offering less and less guidance. Bill was not her child, but he must stand on his own feet, perhaps with a little help, but from a distance. Physically, Bill was a grown man. Mentally, he had above average capacity though he'd explained to her that his gift was not extraordinary intelligence so much as it was an ability and desire to learn — a super focus on those topics and projects that interested him most. Socially, Bill was challenged. He struggled to understand ordinary dynamics and communications between people. In the right environment, perhaps in academia, Bill could flourish. In time, he could adapt to his social disability — maybe through rote memorization of rules applying to common situations. *Was she up to it? Was she both teacher and lover? Could he help to raise children? Would his children struggle the same way?*

He sat, looking at a computer screen. *He probably doesn't fully understand the landscape. He'll muddle around — stepping on toes without knowing it — saying things that are inappropriate.* If she could only follow him around, offering guidance, speaking the unspoken rules of social engagement that most children understand before puberty. It was simply not practical. *How hard it could be!* Yet, there was something about him. An inner strength. An attention to her needs.

Lib waited for someone to open the door. Bill could survive without her.

TONY

He'd seen *DICKENS AND ASSOCIATES* in large letters as they'd exited the elevator. *My luck has changed for the better*, he thought as Lena dropped her purse on the floor of her cubicle, gesturing at a spare chair for him to sit. "Just give me a minute," she said.

Tony sat, watching as Lena logged onto her computer and checked her e-mails. The panic he'd felt earlier was gone. In fact, he felt better than he'd felt in a long time.

"I saw Gerard leBanquier on television."

"Yeah, he's a very nice man," she said, sitting straight in her chair, reading the monitor.

"Where's his office?"

She pointed toward the other end of the room without looking. "He's in the big office in the center."

Tony glanced then turned back, reading over Lena's shoulder — an e-mail from Dirk Dickens with a list of names copied, including Lena Veed. "I get it now," Tony said, recalling her id.

"What?" she asked, typing a response.

"LUV must be your initials."

"Nice work. Yes." She smiled, but didn't turn to face him.

Tony continued to read the names in the cc box. *William Tee*! He felt transported into an episode of the Twilight Zone. "Do you know William Tee?" Tony asked.

"Not really. He's new."

"He works here?"

"Yes, why?"

"I *know* him. Mind if I say hi?"

Lena turned and studied Tony's face for a moment. "Is there something you're not telling me?"

* * *

Tony tapped on the glass door. Bill turned and waved at him to enter.

"*Wow*!" Tony said. "Nice *office*, buddy!"

Bill smiled and shook Tony's hand. "Please sit down."

Dark clouds through the window behind Bill remained a stark contrast to the lighted area in which he sat.

"Why are you here?"

"I know Lena, a girl who works here."

Bill shook his head, indicating he didn't know her.

First a little small talk, maybe build a rapport, then get some answers, Tony thought.

"Anyway, I saw you sittin' here, thought I'd pop in and say hi."

"Hi."

Tony plopped into a chair and played with a magnet toy from Bill's desk. "Have you seen Lib?"

"I talked to her last night on the phone."

"She's not a happy camper."

"She is a happy camper."

"No, Bill, she's *not*."

"I will call her."

"Wait," Tony said. "Let's think through this a bit."

Tony marveled at the magnet toy, swapping it between two hands — his elbows resting on the arms of the chair. He swiveled back and forth a few times, then stopped and looked at Bill.

"You know, Lib's a high maintenance woman."

"Did you hear that?" Bill said.

"Hear *what*?"

"I thought I heard someone cough and clear their throat."

Tony looked over his shoulder, but didn't see anyone. He turned his attention back to Bill. "Anyway buddy, you have to be careful. These chicks can go off like a *bomb*."

Bill's eyes widened at the thought of a chicken exploding in a flash of light, feathers floating alongside charred remains.

"Yeah, you have no idea," Tony continued. "Anyway, I think you're okay though."

"Why am I okay?"

"You know. Because of your condition."

"What do you mean?"

"I mean, Lib's gonna go easy on ya. You don't have to worry."

Bill's eyebrows raised. He stared at Tony's chin, deep in thought.

"I think maybe she feels a little sorry for ya, you lucky dog."

"I do not want to be a lucky dog. I want her to treat me the same . . . well, the same as she would treat a boyfriend or a husband."

"Oh, no, no, no. You know not what you ask for, buddy. It's much better if she gives ya a break."

"If you know so much, why do you not have a girlfriend?"

<snicker>

Tony turned around. "I *heard* that! Who's *in* here?"

A man in a dark suit peered through the glass partition

wall.

"Tony, hang on, I want you to meet my boss, Mr. Dickens."

Bill motioned for Mr. Dickens who promptly stepped inside.

"Mr. Dickens, this is my friend, Tony Wochowski. He's a writer."

"I've seen your articles in the paper. Straight forward. Resolute. I like that." Dickens wrapped his cold fingers around Tony's hand, shaking it a little too slowly for comfort.

"Nice to meet you, sir."

"What brings you here?"

"I saw Lena in the lobby, She told me about your great company."

"Well. I guess she'll get a nice surprise in her next check."

Tony and Dickens laughed.

There's something about him. Tony looked at the scar on Dickens' right eyebrow. It reminded him of something. *What was it?*

"Unfortunate accident. I hit my head on a capstan."

"Sorry. I didn't mean to stare."

Dickens positioned himself in front of Bill's desk.

"It's okay. Happens all the time. Please sit down."

They both sat across from Bill.

"Do you know Lib Rand?" Dickens asked.

"*Know* her? I *work* with her. I'm her mentor."

"I see. Tell me about her."

"First of all, she's drop dead gorgeous."

Dickens nodded his head.

"She's really smart, but she has a violent temper."

"Oh, really?"

"Yeah, I mean, sometimes she can fly off the handle — knock things off shelves — that kinda thing."

Dickens angled his eyes at Bill then back at Tony. "I don't believe you."

"Excuse me?" Tony said.

"I think you're lying."

Bill's eyes widened.

TOM AND GEORGE

"Want some popcorn?" George thrust a red and white striped bag in front of his old friend.

"No thanks."

"Suit yourself, Tommy."

They sat on an early American, plaid couch, in front of a large screen, watching Tony and Bill and Dickens.

Tom wore a tie dyed T -shirt and faded blue jeans. "They just don't get it."

"Yeah, I know."

George shot a glance at his friend, now fumbling with the remote to turn down the sound. "Something tells me you're gonna explain it to me anyway."

"It's all laid out for them, if they'd just follow through."

"Yeah, yeah. It was quite an accomplishment." George reached over, patting Tom on the back.

"They're tearing it all apart Georgie. Everything we worked for, they're letting it go."

"Pipe down old man. Michael's there."

"He's losing control of the situation, can't you see?"

George nodded. "Yeah, we'll soon be outnumbered."

It was part of their daily banter — their fun. George had heard it all, but each version had a slightly different twist — usually related to events displayed on the console monitors or in the larger room where they sat.

Tom removed a small metal box from his jeans. He

lifted the lid, dipping a small spoon inside, and then held it under one side of his nose. He sniffed hard, then repeated the motion for the other side. "A-*choooo*!"

"Nice. All over my knee."

"Sorry." Tom wiped both nostrils with his pinky.

"You know, we were outnumbered before," George said. "It didn't stop us, then."

"I think we've had a nice run, Georgie."

"What?"

"I said, I think we've had a nice run, Georgie!"

Tom hit the pause button.

"That's better," George said. "Pray tell what you mean by that?"

"I mean, how long can a good thing last? Two hundred thirty something years ain't nuthin' to sneeze at."

"Funny."

"Yeah, I try to insert a little humor here and there . . . just to change it up a bit."

"I like the lingo too."

"Yeah, well language is going downhill, too. If you can't beat 'em, join 'em."

"That's not the Tom Jefferson I know."

"Well, I'm tired of worryin' about it Georgie."

George's hand fumbled for popcorn, followed by the sound of his wooden teeth munching and clacking together. An African American woman walked into the large room and sat next to Tom on the couch — patting his leg.

"Good mornin' Sally." George spoke without looking.

"Mornin' Georgie." Sally replied, facing the frozen characters on the screen.

"Tommy here's giving up."

"He not givin' up. He just yankin' yo chain, old fart."

Tom tilted his head to look at George. "I don't know,

Sally. Maybe I should give up. I need some cooperation down there."

George said, "Maybe you're right. The numbers ain't lookin' so good Tom, ol' boy. Maybe you're right."

George grabbed the remote, but Tom held it tight. "I wanna watch Family Feud," George said, tussling over the device.

"Let *go* of it George! I was here *first*. Besides, I wanna see what happened to Donald Trump." Tom and George both slapped at each other with their free hands like kids in the back seat of a car on a long trip, clinging to the remote with their other hand.

"He ain't ded. Dat ol' plastic statue done fell off da roof agin."

"*Excuse* me! *Spoiler* alert!" Tom said before snatching the remote away from George.

"Here, let's see what's going on."

TONY

Tony looked him in the eyes. *There's something about Dickens.* He felt they'd met or maybe he was famous. "I'm taking a beating on my stocks these days," Tony said. "Sure would be nice to find a good advisor."

Dirk smiled and nodded his head. "You might want to go with Edward Jones."

"What about Dickens and Associates?"

"We're a private investment group."

"I can't join?"

Mr. Dickens smiled. "I'm sorry, but no, I don't think so. Come back and see us in a few years."

It felt as though all the oxygen in the room was gone. Feeling small and insignificant, Tony's moment of confidence had faded in the presence of power and influence.

"Well. Look at the time. I think I need to head back over to the *Trib*," Tony said, standing and putting the magnetic toy back on Bill's desk, abandoning his noble mission.

Dickens stood but didn't shake Tony's extended hand which snaked its way back into his jeans pocket.

"I'll talk to you later, buddy," Tony said shakily, moving toward the door before noticing Michael, standing with his arms folded on the other side, blocking his path.

Tony shrugged his shoulders and shook his head. *What*

can I do? he mouthed. To his horror, Michael opened the door and walked in. Dickens stood and turned, his faux smile becoming a thin line on his face.

"Hello, Michael," Dickens said.

"Hello, Dirk."

"You *know* each other?" Tony asked.

"Yeah," they responded in unison.

"We go way back," Michael said without averting his gaze at Dickens, now leaning against Bill's desk. Bill remained seated.

"Excuse me, why are you here?" Bill asked meekly.

"I'm . . . uh . . . here to assist you."

"No, he's not, Bill. He's here to *hurt* you," Dickens said out of the corner of his mouth, maintaining a laser like visage.

"Tony, I think you should leave," Bill said.

"No! I think he should stay and face the music," Dickens said — still glaring at Michael. "Someone else should be here for this."

"Who?" Bill asked.

Dickens' face softened. "Lib? Can you *hear* me? Come out, come out, wher*ever* you are," he sang.

"I'm here." Lib stood between the ficus trees, holding something in her hand.

"How long have you been there?" Tony asked.

"Long enough, my mentor. You better hope I don't launch into a violent *rage*."

Tony covered his face with his hand — fingers spread wide — shaking his head.

"Miss Lib Rand. So nice of you to join us."

Lib stepped away from the wall.

"I'm here to take Bill home."

"Well, Bill's at *work* right now and cannot go home."

"Why's he so important to you?"

Dickens tilted his head.   "He has potential for great things in my organization."

Bill fidgeted in his chair.

"Yes, I agree he has potential. But, I think he can make an informed decision on his own," she said.

Bill looked at Lib then back at Dickens whose eyes remained fixed on Michael. "Why must I choose?"

"Don't be confused, son. It's all smoke and mirrors," Michael offered. "Just watch and listen."

"That's right Bill.   Watch and listen to their empty promises. Who has your back?" Dickens said.

"Hang on. What's this all *about*?" Tony said.

"It's all about our future, cupcake."

"Excuse me? Are you suggesting our future depends on Bill's decision right here in this office?   Right *now*?" Tony said.

"Maybe."

"Okay. I'm confused.   What's he choosing?   Lib or Dickens?"

"More than that, cupcake. Bill's choosing between good and evil."

Bill raised his hand. "May I go to the bathroom?"

"Sit down Bill!" Michael and Dickens shouted in unison.

Bill jiggled his knees for a moment, hands clasped together on his desk, twiddling his thumbs.

TOM AND GEORGE

"What's so special about Bill?" George asked.

"The Big Guy's got plans for 'im. He's gonna do great things, that is, if he isn't devoured by ambition."

"Nothing wrong with ambition," a voice came from the back of the room.

Sally said, "Look who da *cat* done drug in."

"Hey Ben," Tom said. "Wassup?"

"Excuse me?" Franklin looked over his glasses, sipping a glass of Pinot Grigio.

"Kinda *early* for that, eh Ben?" George said.

"It's good for gout."

"We ain't got no gout up *heeah*," Sally teased.

"Well, there you go. And, you wonder why." Ben said.

The others chuckled.

Ben leaned back in a chair and removed his glasses.

"Uh oh." Sally said. "Now we's gonna git a big speech."

George and Tom laughed. Ben cleared his throat.

"Young Master Bill is a student of technology. He'll contribute something of great value to new generations."

"Yeah, like that ol' womanizin' guy from Philly."

"I do not take heed to your slander, Miss Sally. I merely offer that our man has great potential, unrecognized though it may be at the moment."

"He ain't gonna do nuthin'. Those thieves gonna rob

'im blind, leeb 'im on the road fo ded.   You call dat am*bish*un. I calls it *thiev*'ry."

"She's got a point, Ben." Tom said.   "Without enough jobs, folks get nasty."

Ben nodded. "Maybe they could distribute the work more evenly."

Sally said, "You think dem thieves gonna share?   Day ain't sharin' *nuttin*'. Haf da country workin' like field hands on Mr. Tom's plantashun, the udder haf standin' in line fo free biscuits."

"Now, Sally, that was a long time ago."

"I know shuggah. I's just makin' a point."

Tom stood up and stretched his legs.   "Who knew our grand plan for liberty would fall victim to fear and excess and greed and corruption?"

"Hey, it's not over yet," George offered.

TONY

Michael turned to Tony. "Showtime, cupcake."

Tony's mouth gaped open in protest — words could not express.

Michael half winked at him — nodding, urging him to follow his destiny. Tony had no idea. It was off the charts awkward for him. He looked apologetically at Dickens and Bill, searching for the right words. He'd excuse himself and simply walk through the doors to the elevator — back outside. The thunderstorm had subsided and beams of sunlight highlighted several surrounding buildings. *On the count of three. One. Two.*

"He's not a nice man, Bill," Tony said, his eyes wide with fear. "He takes advantage of people who're weak and uses them to carry out his plans."

"What kind of plans?"

"Bernie was one of his guys, isn't that right . . . *Jack*?"

"I don't know who you're talking about," Dirk said.

"I read Bernie's files. He talked about you. He talked about the scar over your eye."

"Lots of people have scars over their eye. My name is Dirk Dickens."

"Where did you say you were *from*, Mr. Dickens?"

"Excuse me?"

Tony hesitated.

"Go on son, finish what you want to say," Michael said.

"Where are you *from*?!" Tony said without thinking. He wanted to leave. It wasn't what he wanted to say.

"That's none of your business."

Looking at Tony and then Dickens, Lib said, "I have a question. You said the markets were down hard, but you said it's all good for Dickens and Associates. Why would you say that?"

"Well," Dickens paused. His eyes darted around, returning to Michael.

"Yeah Dirk, why?" Michael said.

"We often invest on the short side of the market."

"Meaning, you want certain businesses to fail." Tony explained.

"That's correct. It's all perfectly legal."

"I think it's more than that. I think you want the overall economy to fail," Tony said.

Dickens remained resolute. "It's all good for Dickens and Associates."

"What about Bernie?" Lib asked.

"Who's Bernie?"

"Bernie, the security guy you hired. The guy who killed people with a high powered rifle, including the President of the NRA. The guy who detonated an IED at Daley Plaza," Tony said.

I have no idea.

"You *knew* him. I can *prove* it."

"You have no such proof."

"Yes, I *do*. I have communications between the two of you. He kept it all on his computer. I've *read* them."

"It wasn't me. You're mistaken."

"It *was* you. You sent instant messages to him, saying several times, and I quote, 'It's all good for Dickens and Associates.'"

"You people have nothing. My hands are clean."

"Just like the drugs and the prostitutes and the pornography," Tony continued.

Dickens glared at Tony. "You think you have all the answers. You and your high moral standards. Look around. You live in a world of deception."

"It ain't perfect, but nothing's perfect," Lib offered.

"And *you*!" Dickens shifted his gaze momentarily at Lib. "Miss High and Mighty. You want *justice*?! What can *you* do? *Nothing*! You're *pathetic*, trying to convince everyone that you're a champion of the weak and the poor. You know *nothing* about the weak and the poor."

"You may be right," she said defiantly, her eyes sparkling with emotion, "but I don't take advantage of them."

"Anything else you want to say?" Michael asked Tony. Tony hesitated.

"Nice try Michael, but you picked the *wrong boy*." Dickens smirked as he raised his phone and touched the screen.

Michael put his hand on Tony's shoulder.

Tony continued. "Bill, Mr. Dickens doesn't care about you or anybody else. He's not who you think he is and he'll use you until you have nothing left to give." Tony's eyes danced wildly from person to person as he spoke, like tigers prowling from side to side in a cage.

Bill looked at his boss. "I am sorry Mr. Dickens. I do not know what is going on."

"Let me handle this, Bill." Dickens spoke calmly into the phone, "Security breach, Action 5." He put the device back into his pocket and folded his arms.

Tony pointed through the glass wall into the open office area where several employees stood, talking while occasionally glancing over at Bill's office. "If you won't tell Bill, these people will tell him what you're up to."

"No, they won't. Trust me."

"Trust *you*? You *cannot* be trusted." Tony stepped toward the door.

"*Stop!*" Dickens' voice filled the space, causing Lib to jump.

A small plane pulling a banner made it's way through the remaining clouds. Tony's curiosity drove him to watch through the window as the message appeared. *STOP WORRYING. THINGS WILL WORK OUT IN THE END.*

Wobbling a bit, the plane banked and headed for the window behind Bill.

"Oh, *shit!*" Tony said.

Everyone looked as the plane continued to wobble. It banked hard to the right, then disappeared into a ball of flame, crashing into the top two floors of the building across the river, the banner floating down alongside.

"Bill you're in great danger," Tony said, watching the flames shooting from two-hundred yards away. *What the hell is going on?* he thought.

"Bill, you're not in danger. These people are trying to confuse you. Please sit down."

Bill looked at Lib with puppy dog eyes then sat, glancing over his shoulder at the plane hanging from the building.

Tony opened the door and addressed the crowd. "The work you're doing is evil. Mr. Dickens is using you all, it's a scam."

"Think about what you're doing, Tony. You're making a big mistake."

"He's responsible for the pandemonium," Tony continued.

"No, it's all good for Dickens and Associates! Go back to work!" Dirk shouted to the employees from inside Bill's office.

Several employees broke off — walking slowly back to their cubicles. The others remained — including Lena.

"Okay, Tony," Dickens said. "Think about Lena. What'll happen to her?"

Standing with arms wrapped around herself, she looked confused and frightened. He wanted to go on a dinner date with her. He would apologize for his behavior and be on his way.

"Lena, Dirk Dickens is a monster," Tony blurted. "He's poisoning the minds of the people you bring to him. He builds on their fear and their anger, hoping to cash in when things go bad. The guys in the offices?" Tony pointed at Mr. leBanquier and several other executives, now gathered outside their offices. "The guys in the offices are attacking the markets as we speak. They're all under his spell, Lena. You can make a difference. You can choose the right path. Walk away. Walk away now and I'll help you find a better job, working for someone you can trust."

One of the executives glared at leBanquier and then abruptly turned and walked back inside an office.

"I believe you," Lena said softly. She turned to the others standing around. "I believe him," She said, using a finger to wipe under one eye. "I'm leaving and I think you all should leave, too."

She looked at Tony and waved the fingers of one hand at him before turning toward the elevators. Several folks talked, then two followed. The others seemed hesitant.

"You're doing the right thing, Lena," Tony called after her.

Tony turned and addressed the others. "He makes you

call them, doesn't he?   What do you give them, hope or desperation?   Do you shine a light on their injustice — leading them further down the road of self pity and negativity?   Who *are* they?   They're the *weak*.   They need something positive in their lives.   Instead, you give them justification for their anger and their frustration.   You empower them to take it upon themselves, responding in a *negative* way rather than a *positive* way.   You deliver them into Dickens' hands.   Do you know what he asks them to do?   He wants to destroy freedom.   He wants to destroy our country — our way of life.   In exchange for what?   It's all good for Dickens and Associates, right?   Have you heard that before?   Ever wonder why he says it when things are going bad?   *Think* about it!"

"That's e*nough*!" Dirk roared.   They *need* me.   I'm their benefactor.   I pay them well and they're *loyal* to me!

Several more employees walked toward the elevators, shaking their heads.   They passed three men in jump suits, on their way to Bill's office.

The men in jump suits grabbed Tony's arm and wrestled him to the floor as he released the glass door, allowing it to close.   Tony could see Lib and Bill and Michael, watching as the uniformed men cuffed him.   He felt a needle in his arm.   He saw Lib . . . watching . . . watching.   Michael opened the door and spoke.   "You'll be okay, cupcake," his distorted voice echoed, trailing behind.

LIB

"Is he okay?" Lib said.

"I think he'll be fine." Dirk responded, leaning back against Bill's desk.

"He's dead," Michael said.

"No he's not."

Lib glared at Dirk. "Who *were* those guys?"

"I have no earthly idea, really."

"I think something is wrong here," Bill said, his eyes red. He looked at Lib then Dirk.

"Bill. Listen to me," Lib began. "You're *right*. *None* of this makes sense. Please, come with me. Let's go home."

"Don't move, Bill. You cannot go home now. You *are* home."

"I believe in him, too," Bill said.

"Who?" Lib and Michael said in unison.

"Tony."

"Okay, I'll just make another call," Dirk said.

"Wait a minute, *Jack*! *Two* can play that game." Michael fished a phone out of his pocket. "I'll call a few of *my* people."

Dirk put his phone down. He extended his hands on both sides — an apparent gesture of peace. "Michael, Michael. I'm just kidding. Let's be reasonable, shall we?"

Michael pressed a button on his phone and waited. "I get so tired of this same scene. We come face to face.

People get murdered. You go away. You come back. You call your people. I call my people, who always outnumber your people. I'm ready for retirement." He turned to face the wall with the phone in his hand. "It's time," he said.

TONY

An instrumental version of "The Girl From Ipanema" played over an intercom. Tony stood in a long, white corridor behind an older man and woman who were both badly burned. "Are you okay?" he asked.

"Sam had a heart attack. We were supposed to fly over Wrigley Field with a banner, then a huge thunderstorm came out of nowhere."

Tony nodded.

"When the clouds cleared, I realized where I was and tried to make a turn. There were buildings in every direction," Sam explained. "Then, my chest tightened. I don't remember much after that."

"Stop worrying. Everything will work out in the end," Tony said.

"Wow," Sam said, "that's what was on the banner."

Tony smiled. Scores of people stood in line. Two wore police uniforms. One wore a hospital gown. The man behind him was naked, all except his socks.

"What happened to you?"

"Doctor gave me Viagra. The first one didn't do anything. The second one helped a little. I took the whole bottle."

"How'd that work out for you?"

"It was great. Had 'ol Dixie singin' 'Row Row Row Your Boat'."

"Who's Dixie?"

"She's my girlfriend at Shady Acres. Well, she *was* my girlfriend."

"So, whatja do?"

"Well, I was having so much fun, I started singin' too."

"Row Row Row Your Boat?"

"No. I started singin' Dixieland. 'Oh, I wish I were in Dixie, hooray, hooray! In Dixieland I'll make my stand . . . to live and die in Dixie!'" It was like in grammar school when you sing two songs together. We were having a good ol' time!"

Tony smiled. "So, *then* what happened?"

"Nurse came in and started to yellin' at us. I'm like, 'close the *door* fool!! Can't you see I'm *busy*!' Well, she runs down the hall, leavin' the door wide open as our friends gathered around on walkers and wheelchairs, whoopin' and a hollerin' and a cheerin' us on."

Tony chuckled.

The old man continued, "Well, I'm holding on to those rails, ya know, for balance. Nurse comes back in and releases one of 'em. It drops down and I just fall right offa ol' Dixie down onto the floor, hittin' my head on an IV stand."

The man turned and showed Tony a gash on the side of his head.

Tony folded his arms, waiting. He looked at his watch, patting his foot to an "Up Up And Away" instrumental played on steel drums.

TOM

"The original Constitution wasn't perfect," Tom said.

Abe shifted in his chair. "No, you're right, but we fixed it."

Tom shook his head. "Well, it's still not perfect, but it's better than tyranny or chaos."

"They're losing it," Abe said. "Justice has been lost to corruption."

"It's not just justice, Abe, it's about balance of control. In their attempts to address every corner of society, they're tipping the scales."

"I'm afraid you're right," Abe said, resting his bearded chin on his folded hands.

"The national debt is out of control," Tom continued. "Kids are killing each other in the streets. The prisons are full. Businesses and foreign governments are paying for policy. The Middle Class is shrinking. People are angry and restless. It's a *mess* down there."

"Shut up, you two," George said. "I wanna see what happens next."

"Whad I miss?" Tony asked, closing the door behind him.

"Ol Michael doin' it again, disarming Dirk," Sally said.

"What about Lib?"

"She makin' googly eyes at Bill. They's gonna be a happy couple."

"What's gonna happen to the employees who stay? What's gonna happen to Dirk?"

"Shhhhh! Be quiet."

BILL

The few remaining employees standing outside Bill's office made their way back to their desks, including Cherise and Mr. Jepson. Bill looked at the phone on his desk, reading the options. Intercom #5. He lifted the phone receiver and pressed #5, then placed the magnet toy in the cradle before lowering the receiver down gently, resting on the magnet toy, just above the button.

Dirk stared at Lib. "I like your piece," he said.

"Excuse me?"

He smiled at her. "The article you wrote."

Lib glared back at him. "I don't care."

Dirk shifted his weight, standing a little taller — a perfect gentleman, harmless. "I've been looking for someone like you. I have just the job, complete with all the perks."

Lib folded her arms.

"I cannot decide on a title. Maybe Communications Director. Better yet. Maybe Vice President of Communications."

Lib said nothing.

Dirk held one elbow with his hand, the other hand cradling his chin. He seemed to study Lib, like someone regarding the value of a painting. "I could offer a nice signing bonus."

Lib's expression softened a bit.

"I'm thinking $500K, but I cannot be convinced to go further . . ." his voice trailing briefly, " . . . than say, $750K."

Michael leaned against the opposite wall, watching, waiting.

Lib looked at Bill. "That's a lot of money to offer someone you don't know."

"Oh, I know you better than you think. It's possible I know you a little better than you know yourself."

"Will you put it in writing?"

"*No!*" Bill blurted.

Dirk turned and glared at Bill. "You're . . . " he took a deep breath, again demonstrating patience and understanding — a compassionate father speaking to a child. "You should think about what you're saying, young man. The two of you might enjoy yourselves. Don't let a great opportunity slip past."

Lib cleared her throat. Dickens turned back to her, smiling, encouraging her to speak.

"What would I do?"

"Ah. That's a very good question. First of all, I'm easy. I want to create a collaborative environment. Of course, at the end of the day, I must make the final decision. But, you're an intelligent, beautiful woman. You can help others to understand."

"Understand *what*?"

"This is a nasty, competitive world. They can do something to change it. I'm talking about a network of high quality people such as yourself, working toward common goals."

Lib looked at Bill, then back at Dirk.

Michael looked at Lib. "Don't be fooled, toots. Things aren't always as they seem."

"Don't listen to that ol' coot. You may want to ask him

about his stay at Gateway," Dirk said.

"It was an assignment."

"Right. You took that role rather seriously, did you not? Complete with delirium tremors and psychosis. Isn't that what the report said?"

Bill looked at Michael who remained semi-slumped against the wall, arms folded, stone faced. He glanced at Bill and shrugged it off before returning his attention to Dirk and Lib.

Lib continued. "Tony said you're involved in drugs and prostitution."

"Oh no. I have nothing to do with drugs or prostitution. Some of my *clients* may be involved with those things."

"Clients?"

"People who need my help. I offer them prosperity."

"I'm still a little confused. You seem genuinely happy when the world is falling apart at the seams."

"Again, I'm a businessman. I follow the trends. As a shareholder, you will soon learn to trust my judgment. What's good for Dickens and Associates will be good for you too."

"Such as?"

"Whatever. If things go well, we make a profit. If people fight in the streets, we make a profit. If war breaks out, we make a profit."

Lib looked down at the carpet.

"Nice work, Dirk," Michael said. "Casting doubt again."

Dickens smiled. "They listen because they know what I'm talking about. People waste so much time and energy pretending to care. The only real, sustainable charity is through strength — seizing opportunity when it's available. You know that as well as I do, Michael."

"I agree. At least, I agree that's the message of the world."

Lib looked back at Michael. "You haven't said much. I wanna hear *your* thoughts."

"Well. I don't have a fancy office or fancy clothes, but I can offer something perhaps a bit closer to home."

"Meaning?"

"You asked a question recently."

"I don't recall."

"You were trying to understand the balance between tyranny and liberty."

"Well, yes, but I didn't ask you that."

"Liberty cannot exist without order. It's a big lie, just like this guy. Think about what he's offering. He doesn't care about anything, except maybe himself. He thrives on unrest. He thrives on chaos and destruction. He wants to remind people of their most basic needs beyond the needs of others."

"And, Michael," Dirk offered calmly, "what's so wrong with *that*?"

"You *are* disorder. You play both sides. You love hatred. You love prisons. You love gangs and corruption in government. You love bullying. You love all forms of extremism, no matter *which* side. It's about creating unrest and if I might offer a compliment, you're very good at it."

"Thank you." Dickens still looked at Michael, unfazed by his allegations. "You're such an idealist. All this talk. The next thing, you'll talk about love and compassion and we can all hug in the middle of the room."

"Maybe."

"It's a game. It's all good for Dickens and Associates. Sure, I love attitudes of superiority. I love conflict without resolution. You're right. I love extremism in all forms. So what?"

"Just look around, Lib," Michael said. "You don't wanna live in a world in which drugs are universally accepted. You don't want survival of the fittest. Your Dad's a gentle man. He loves you and he loves justice."

On the other side of the glass wall, Cherise and a few other folks walked toward the elevator, some carrying boxes, others just a briefcase or a purse.

Michael put a cigarette in his mouth. "Gotta light?"

"Sure." Dirk extended his forefinger, a small flame appearing at the tip.

"Thanks."

"Don't mention it."

Lib's eyes widened.

LIB

They all watched smoke billowing from the building across the river.

"Michael, do you have any idea how long it takes to organize people these days?" Dirk asked, his hands folded behind his back.

"I hope a long time."

"Actually, not very long at all. People welcome me with open arms."

"I'm gettin' old."

"Perhaps you're right. Maybe it's too much for you. Maybe send a younger man who can keep up." Dirk smiled.

"What will you do, Michael?" Lib asked.

"I don't know, hang out with old friends. Maybe go to a ball game."

"Well, I hope the next guy is as much fun as you," Dirk offered.

"Yeah. I hope the next guy sends you back where you belong."

Michael headed for the door.

Lib asked, "Who are you, really?"

"I'm Bill's guardian angel. You're just along for the ride, toots. There may be hope for you, yet."

"That's what my daddy called me."

"I know."

"Where're you going?" she asked.

"I'm going back for a little R&R before my next assignment."

"What about me and Bill?"

"You'll be fine. You get it. Bill gets it. The employees get it. See?" He pointed. "They're all leaving." They stood, waiting for the elevator, all except Mr. Jepson, waiting patiently on his master.

"Security will escort you out. Without his minions, this guy has nothing to work with. See ya on the other side."

Two police officers and a security guard exited the elevator, passing Michael who turned and waved at Lib and Bill. Dirk waved too. Michael flipped him the finger and followed the remaining employees who'd boarded the elevator, exhaling cigarette smoke as the doors closed.

LIB
Three Months Later

"So, what's a good name for a boy?" Lib asked.

"How about Tony?" Bill said.

"How 'bout Michael?"

They looked at each other for a moment before shaking their heads no.

"How about Russ?" Lib suggested.

"I get it. Russ Tee."

"How about Oppa Tuna?" Lib said, giggling.

"That's ridiculous."

Sitting on the front porch of Lib's family farm in Lowell, Indiana, Bill picked up the Tribune. Lib's mother's voice drifted through the screen door, singing an old hymn from the kitchen. Two thousand acres of corn stood firmly against the breeze. Maybe Billy could run the harvester, Lib thought.

She rocked, listening to the deck boards and the creaking of the chair on a perfect sort of day — a day without calamity, without pandemonium.

"I thought we'd reached the end of the world," Lib said.

"Yes, me too. But, I'm still not sure."

"Why do you say that?"

"The Cubs won the World Series last night," Bill said, holding up the front page of the Chicago Tribune.

"I *told* you they would."

Bill leaned over from the porch swing and poked LIb's tummy. "You hear that Bill Jr.?, Cubs won!"

He leaned back and flipped a few pages. "You think you'll miss working at the *Trib*?"

"I don't know . . . I guess I'll find out soon enough."

"Maybe you can finish your book."

"What? And let you do all the fun stuff around here?"

"I've been up since five this morning. I'll admit, it's not easy but it feels good."

"You'll still have time to work on your new inventions."

"Okay, okay."

"Dinner'll be ready in ten minutes!" Lib's mother called from inside.

"How's the micro power plant coming along?" Lib asked.

"Good. It's a patentable idea."

"Tell me again, what's the benefit?"

"It reduces demand with point of use power generation."

"I guess I don't get it."

"The idea is to provide power at the place where it's needed. Transmitting power is not very efficient."

"What about superconducting power lines?"

"Superconducting power lines help cut down power distribution losses, true. But, they are not practical on a large scale, requiring massive cooling systems, another drain on power."

"I hope your idea works."

"Me too."

A breeze blew from the southwest, rustling the leaves, accompanying the sounds of rocker and porch swing keeping time.

"Hey Lib."

"What?"

"Here's your opinion piece."
"It's a little heavy."
"Like you?"
"Funny. Very. Funny."

SAVE THE MIDDLE CLASS
By Lib R. Tee

Arianna Huffington wrote, "It's no longer an exaggeration to say that middle-class Americans are an endangered species." I agree, though I wonder if folks realize the importance of the middle class.

It's simple. Without a middle class, there's little cash flow. America's a great consumer nation — an economy built primarily on our ability to purchase goods and services. It's about jobs and spending. Without domestic demand, there's less supply, resulting in lay-offs and unrest. Please keep in mind, rich folks spend only a small percentage of their income on goods and services while poor folks don't have the money to spend.

Ultimately, the relative size of our middle class is a single measure of liberty and justice, demonstrating balance in our society. Yet the message seems lost in the noise created by extremism. We should all work to preserve the middle class, no matter where we exist in the economic spectrum.

As a nation, we're responding poorly. Our leaders respond with rhetoric while people react — venting their frustrations online — a form of mass hysteria. We've become a nation of extremists — our news delivered daily in two distinct flavors — liberal and conservative. Indeed, pointing fingers has become the solution of the day in our culture. We look for someone to blame while standing in ideological corners, further and further from the middle — the place best representing our collective interests. Without the middle, there's no opportunity for the rich and eventually, there's no basis for protecting the poor.

But much has changed over the past fifty years. For example, lobbyists are more powerful than ever, with private money flowing into political coffers like water over Niagara Falls. At the same time, our government continues to grow at an alarming rate. In essence, today's political parties represent the interests of big business and big government on opposite ends of a spectrum that has become noticeably void in the middle. We wonder what's wrong with our kids, perhaps without taking the time to look at ourselves, our collective behavior and our leadership. We can address individual symptoms or we can look for a fundamental root cause permeating all levels of society — a common thread. I believe the common thread is extremism.

On a fundamental level, perhaps we should look at why our political process rewards excess rather than moderation.

My political science professor once explained it using the reflecting pool analogy. It's a representation of how the majority of American voters figuratively wade back and forth in the manmade body of water located between the Lincoln Memorial representing a compassionate government and the Washington Monument representing strength. The idea is that we'll slowly and deliberately achieve the balance necessary to sustain our way of life.

If the Lincoln Memorial represents compassion and the Washington Monument represents strength, perhaps the symbol for the middle class is the reflecting pool itself. Maybe it's time for the embattled middle class to set up residence between extreme ideologies. Maybe it's time to take a stand . . . in the middle. Maybe it's time for moderation to establish an identity — a full time residence worthy of supporting rather than a whistle stop on the road between extremes.

When Wall Street and big government are given priority, we lose the center of our existence. We've already lost most of our manufacturing base, including multiple supply chains and services supporting the most basic element of our economy. Our ability to build products using our own workforce represents not only the means to produce goods, but also the means to consume goods. In essence, our workers are the fuel for the domestic economy.

The poor and the rich have their representation with today's Democrats and Republicans — both clearly tied to interests that no longer align with the middle. So, who has the basic needs of the middle class at the top of their agenda? Must we pay money to get someone's attention?

Meanwhile, those with a stake in the old guard will not go quietly into submission. They'll resist and they'll create barriers. But, I believe moderates are not interested in revolution in the traditional sense. We want representation and justice while preserving our basis for democracy — the political equivalent of the Hippocratic oath, to do no harm.

In the meantime, extremism remains a threat to our way of life.

TOM

"Michael! How was your vacation?" Tom asked.

"Buncha tourists with whiny kids." Michael retrieved a cigarette from behind his ear, poking it into the corner of his mouth.

"Uh, Michael. Have you forgotten?" Tom asked.

Michael shifted his weight. "You know, they allow smoking in the *other* place," the cigarette dancing on his lips as he spoke.

"Not that. *Attitude*, Michael. It's all about *attitude*."

"I'm trying."

"Nothing can stop the man with the *right* mental attitude from achieving his goal; nothing on earth can help the man with the *wrong* mental attitude," Tom said. "It's the same here. We have a standard to uphold."

"I just don't like people very much, okay?"

"Most folks are as happy as they make up their minds to be," Abe said. "You want another assignment?"

"Okay, okay. Give me a break. How's it going with Lib and Bill?" Michael asked, changing the subject.

The three ex-Presidents, Tom, George and Abe, sat with Ben, chairs in a semicircle around a fire.

Abe scratched his beard. "I think those two will be fine."

"Oh, I hope so, honey," Sally called from her position on the couch, sewing a quilt and watching the screen.

Ben sat, looking over his glasses, his hands folded on his belly. "I think they're fine, but I'm not so sure about the country."

The roaring fire had reduced to small flames, flickering around a smoldering pile of charred logs — a faint red glow deep inside.

"I never thought we'd end up with four branches of government," Tom said, stoking the fire.

"Four?" George answered, "There's only *three*."

Tom shook his head. "Nope. Four. Lobbyists now represent a de facto fourth branch."

"I thought you liked the idea of an aristocratic society making important decisions?"

"A guy can change. I'm kinda leaning more toward the middle these days. A wise man once said, 'I hope we shall crush in its birth the aristocracy of our monied corporations which dare already to challenge our government to a trial by strength, and bid defiance to the laws of our country.'"

Abe stood up and stretched. He bent his lanky frame and retrieved a log, then tossed it on the fire.

"Oh no. Here *he* go," Sally teased.

"Nearly all men can stand adversity, but if you want to test a man's character, give him power," Abe said. "As I would not be a slave, so I would not be a master. This expresses my idea of democracy though we the people are the rightful masters of both Congress and the courts, not to overthrow the Constitution but to overthrow the men who pervert the Constitution."

"Hear, hear!" Ben returned to his pipe, puffing to keep it lit.

Abe continued. "Besides, I get uneasy when people grow restless."

"Understandable. Completely understandable. We

should talk to the boss about it." Tom said.

Michael sat next to Tony at a table on the opposite side of the room. "I've got one for you," Tony said.

"Let's hear it cupcake."

"We will never have true civilization until we have learned to recognize the rights of others."

The men looked at each other. Ben shrugged. "Who said that?"

"Will Rogers."

A clock had been placed on the mantle, a reminder of their past. The perpetual ticking marked the timelessness, providing a frame of reference for those struggling to let go of the material world, much the same way in which many had struggled to embrace the spiritual world from the other side. The clock, like the fire and the food and the drink, had no real function. It served only as an aesthetic, a nostalgic accessory. The clock and the fire represented only one of many scenes in which their souls found comfort, some seeking the familiar, others seeking adventure, all seeking love and acceptance.

LIB

"Hmmmmm."

"What's wrong?" Lib asked.

"You're changing."

"I suppose so. A lot has happened."

Bill lightly scuffed his shoes on the porch decking, keeping time with the rhythmic groaning of the chain.

"Was it Bernie?"

"Excuse me?"

"Did the situation with Bernie influence you?"

Lib rocked double time with the porch swing, looking out across the corn. It really was a perfectly nice day, but cooler nights were a harbinger for the months ahead.

"I guess I've struggled to resolve my response to him. I can't stop thinking about it."

"He didn't give you a choice."

"But, our laws don't support my actions. I was in his house. I entered unlawfully. I killed him and we covered it up."

"Still Lib, you said it yourself, he didn't deserve to live."

"It's not my place. I took it upon myself to take his life. Where does it end? I mean, if we all try to control our environment, think what it might look like."

Bill nodded.

"Yet, there's a need for controls in our society. I'm beginning to realize it in a very different way than before.

Maybe it's because we're gonna be parents. Besides, I don't want to judge and condemn people at a moment's notice. Our system of justice has that responsibility, as long as it remains intact. We've got enough attitudes of superiority as it is, without folks gettin' into each other's business."

"I agree."

"Don't take this the wrong way, Billy, but you and Bernie are alike in some ways. He had potential, just like you, but he chose an evil path. He let it get to him. On the other side, think about a society obsessed with protecting themselves from evil. Think about Mayor Epstein and his response. You were lumped into a group of people, though you'd done nothing. Ironically, the same dragnet failed to catch Bernie. Creating safety for our citizens has a limit. Too much is too much. At some point, an overabundance of law can actually hurt our system of justice."

"You know, I wonder sometimes if maybe we should take care that we don't become part of the same world the Apostle Paul warned us about."

"Exactly. Tyranny creates hardships for people. On the opposite end, our privileges, when taken too far, begin to encroach on the rights of others." Lib shook her head slowly. "I don't want folks walkin' down the street naked or having sex in public. At some point, our privileges must be restricted in deference to the rights of others. This is a problem in our society. How do we draw a line, fairly representing the greater good?"

"What changed your mind about politics?"

"In college, I'd convinced myself that extreme positions were necessary to swing the pendulum back toward the middle."

"You took an extreme position."

"Right. Just like the porch swing, you cannot affect

motion from the middle. You swing in the opposite direction. Our government operates the same way."

"There's a 'but' in there somewhere."

"But, nobody impacts change from the center. We impact change from the opposite position."

"Does it work?"

"It did. At least, until recently."

"What happened?"

"*Money* happened. Political *power* happened. Now, the people have much less influence over policy, so it doesn't shift based solely on our concerns. Instead, it's the influence of the whole world — foreign governments and corporations and PACs and special interest groups. This is a big problem for our government."

"I get the problem with extremes, but how do we protect folks without addressing particular needs?"

"You mean, like creating specific rights for everyone?"

"Well, yes."

"Our basic rights are covered by the Constitution. Beyond that, it's impossible to address every corner of society without creating voids in the process. Eventually, we find ourselves embroiled in legality, creating specific classes of people, measuring rights and privileges by what people don't have rather than what they do have."

Bill nodded his head.

Lib continued. "At some point, we must rely on the compassion of people, not the courts. Otherwise, we must make every exception. Sadly, the least among us suffer when our good intentions exceed the capacity of our court system, attempting to level the playing field. A strong middle class levels the playing field, offering opportunity for those who fuel our economy, requiring a less contentious environment."

"Then on the other side, we struggle to maintain balance in our free enterprise system." Bill added.

"Right. The crash in 2008 is a great example. Everyone blamed negligent lending practices, but the failure was far bigger."

"I remember that. We bailed out some banks and insurance companies."

"Right," Lib said, her eyes sparkling. "Too big to fail. We reacted out of fear that it would drag down the world economy. We're talking about homes in America — a market not big enough to drag down the world economy. It was also the unregulated derivatives markets."

"I know about derivatives. It's like placing bets on the movement of stocks, commodities and currency."

"Correct." Lib shifted in the rocker. "Even back then, I'd begun to doubt the idea that a market could regulate itself naturally. Greenspan had something to say about it. The derivatives markets grew larger than the world economy and companies who'd insured the investments with credit default swaps began to collapse. It was like pulling a box of cereal from the bottom of a pyramid display at the grocery store, the bottom box representing individual mortgages. On top of individual mortgages were mortgage backed securities. On top of mortgage backed securities were insurance policies, called credit default swaps, written to protect investors against loss. Taking out the box at the bottom resulted in a chain reaction in an already unstable system, far larger than the American mortgage market alone."

"I like the cereal reference," Bill said. "It reminds me how we met, though, somehow, falling cereal boxes don't seem that bad."

Lib smiled. "Oh, it's *bad* all right. In 2010, after the crash, the derivatives market was $1.2 quadrillion. World

GDP on the other hand, was only $62 trillion." Tapping her iPhone, Lib used a calculator app. "The derivatives market was 19 times larger than the whole world economy in 2010."

"That's absurd."

"Tell me about it. I once thought market forces were enough to maintain the balance but I began to realize the need for regulations and controls."

"Aha. So you started to move away from your libertarian position."

"Now I'm a moderate." Lib smirked, then said, "I have zero representation."

They continued to swing in time, feeling the breeze.

"What about Dickens?" Bill asked.

"What about him?"

"When will he organize another group of people?"

"I suspect he's already at work. We'll always have evil, even when disguised as something good, playing on our fears."

"Like Dickens and Associates."

"Right. I think Churchill was correct. 'The only thing to fear is fear itself.' Nothing scares me more than people who are scared."

"I'm scared of clowns."

Bill genuinely looked fearful.

"Whatever."

Lib shifted her body in the rocker. The additional weight pressed on her bladder.

"I'm a little scared right now, but I'm looking forward to becoming a mother."

"It will all work out. Everything changes over time."

"I want to live in a world in which *a Billy Tee* isn't crushed by corruption, power and blind ambition."

"Me too."

"Meanwhile, our crime problem is a symptom of something far more dangerous. Maybe folks will connect the dots before it's too late. If not, we're in for some really strange stuff. But, you know what Mayor Daley said about the Picasso statue, don't you?"

"What?"

"We dedicate this celebrated work this morning with the belief that what is strange to us today will be familiar tomorrow."

AUTHOR'S NOTES

I wrote Homeland Insecurity as part of the NaNoWriMo competition in November of 2013. It began with a half dozen flawed characters and a premise -- domestic terrorism set in Chicago, perhaps representing a sad reality for the families of children murdered in the streets almost every day.

Nonetheless, I hope my story is entertaining.

For the second time in two attempts at fiction, I enjoyed a period of discovery as the characters responded to conditions I'd laid before them. I've since grown to love them -- not for *what* they represent, but *how*. They delivered.

Bill represents a unique blend of skill and imperfection as an "Aspie." Though Asperger's Syndrome is rare, all humans possess strengths and weaknesses. Bill also represents innocence. In this setting, Bill functions well in his particular niche, but he's vulnerable to a sometimes overly competitive and paranoid society.

Lib starts out as a libertarian, but she changes. Michael tells her that liberty is not possible without order. On a larger scale, I attempt to demonstrate our collective need for balance.

Tony, Bernie, Michael and Dirk are all straight forward in their representations.

Though the conditions are also extreme, I hope my story presents relevant topics from a fairly neutral point of view. My personal concern is with extremism, so I'm really not fully aligned with the far left or far right, though my neighbors in Illinois may call me a staunch conservative while my friends and family in Georgia may think I'm a liberal. Such is life for a moderate.

Like my characters, I discovered several themes as well, surpassing my original intent. One theme is the ideological polarization of American society (a form of extremism) on a variety of levels. Another theme is the impact of extremism, particularly on the economy, also represented through the over-the-top style in which Homeland is written. Of course, there's the overwrought "good vs. evil" theme, perhaps resembling what I've observed -- that is, good and evil are not always clear.

I think most folks like to discover for themselves, so I resisted the urge to explain, leaving much to the reader's imagination and discretion, if I'm so lucky to actually have readers. In truth, I wanted to say more to help connect-the-dots for my intended market, perhaps only consisting of my wife and one sympathetic relative. If I can help them to understand, I told myself, maybe they might offer a reasonable defense should someone later mischaracterize my intentions, no doubt labeling me a menace to society. Of course, for that to happen, I must have more than two readers, so I'm probably safe.

What more would I say? I wanted to more clearly connect our crime issues to the loss of opportunity which I attribute to extremism. How? Well, first of all, I wanted to demonstrate how extremism is killing small business in America. I think it's clear, but my reality may not be the reader's reality. As proof, I might offer data to support that small business (less than 500 employees) is shrinking in the U.S. as a percentage of GDP, or show a tendency toward increasing regulations and taxes, or a disturbing trend toward larger corporations at the expense of "mom and pop shops", but sadly it would only speak to those who are predestined to believe it in the first place.

I wanted to offer a solution to the problem on the other end of the economic spectrum with derivatives markets, suggesting a way to shift the tax burden onto this form of legalized gambling -- away from the Middle Class, that is, if tax burdens are ever shifted away from *anything*. Think about it. Derivatives markets are 15 to 19 times the size of world GDP, and they're not paying their fair share of taxes, so we pound small businesses comprising most of our Middle Class? Why? I guess because we can.

Offering data to support my beliefs doesn't fit into fiction. It's distracting, and for many . . . well . . . boring. I could present additional correlations with charts such as the U.S. incarceration rate -- number one in the world -- to show how we're moving further toward a police state. I could show the reduction in manufacturing jobs and tons of data showing how the Middle Class is declining. I could argue that lost opportunity is directly tied to criminal activity. That is, when people are hungry, they will find ways to survive.

I could demonstrate that we're all unique in our systems of belief, including our opinions on issues about which we typically answer in one of two ways. Either we support a particular issue or we're against it. When we line up all of the possible issues in our country, it becomes increasingly unlikely that any two of us will agree on each and every issue. That's the whole point. We're unique. Yet, our political system is represented by two ideological entities, each seeking to destroy the other while leaving a noticeable void in the middle. Somehow, many feel compelled to align themselves 100% with extreme ideologies which remain unproven.

I wanted Bill to describe our tendency toward extremism in mathematical terms. I wanted him to demonstrate how ridiculous it is for our government and our society to divide ourselves into only two bundles of policies. My formula? 2^n. Two (2) represents two possible answers of either "yes" or "no" in the form of a "one (1)" or a "zero (0)" to any particular issue while "n" represents the number of issues. So, what does it say? It says, as the number of issues increase, the number of possible combinations (representing individuals), should be larger than only two sets of extreme policies. In other words, the Middle Class needs better representation. Mathematically, today's Democrats and Republicans may be hypothetically represented as all "ones" or all "zeros" -- entrenched on opposite ends, seemingly unwilling to compromise for the greater good of our country.

Okay, charts are one thing, but formulas? I'm really treading on thin ice here. By the way, why haven't the great writers of our day discovered the effectiveness of math in presenting a particular point of view? Tom Clancy, maybe. I suppose it doesn't lend itself to the social context that we enjoy in fiction. It becomes more like a technical manual from the 70's -- which is why I left it out of the story and placed it at the back of the book where only half of my intended market (half of two is one) may look -- most likely the sympathetic relative. My poor wife has heard all this before. Nonetheless, I think my formulaic characterization of our current trend toward extremism demonstrates an important point. Again, the Middle Class needs better representation.

Okay, enough about gastroenterology.

On the subject of genre, I'm aware of the risk when blurring the lines that distinguish story types. I know I can write a straight-up, genre story. But, I also know that it's all been done before. Sure, I might add a twist here or there, or maybe develop a style all my own. With a little luck, I might create a character who may be used over and over again in a series. But, that's not what this is. Besides, so *what* if I have ghosts in my political thriller that's also a satire? Fine, though self publishing may be my only option.

Finally, I leave it to the reader to decide. Ultimately, I hope that it will encourage someone, anyone, to think for themselves on a number of relevant topics. I hope maybe one additional person might realize what we're doing to ourselves. Maybe one person will have the courage to stand up for what is right rather than follow the status quo.

Del Boland

SHAMELESS PROMOTION PAGE

Coming soon from the slightly twisted mind of Del Boland . . .

Exposed Shorts: A Collection of Short Stories

Eggbert: An Alien Memoir

Answering Common Objections to God

Box of Dreams - After the death of his son, Art discovers an ancestral diary written in code. He's seduced by an old girlfriend and targeted by a mysterious enemy while racing to unlock the code, hoping to find lost Confederate Gold.